The Tycoon's Forced Bride

A Bad Boy Short Romance

Jane Porter

TULE
PUBLISHING

Dedication

For my amazing, loyal readers who know (and embrace!) that I don't always write nice, normal romances, featuring lovely, well-adjusted characters who meet while shopping for organic produce.

This one, dear readers, is for you…

Chapter One

H E KNEW AVA'S daily routine down to the minute.

It wasn't a difficult routine to learn. She never varied her routine. It was the same Monday through Friday. A car picked her up promptly at eight ten for work. She was at her desk at the ballet school by eight thirty. She taught two classes before she had lunch at her desk, and then two more in the afternoon, in between meetings with the school and company.

The same town car that dropped her off in the morning returned at six to collect her. Back home, she rarely went out in the evenings. She rarely ordered food for delivery. On weekends she stayed in, except for the special evening where she attended a performance, and, then again, she traveled in the town car, arriving a full hour and a half before the performance to give her time to get into the theater before the crowds arrived, and then returning a full hour after, when the crowds had dispersed. It wasn't just because she moved slowly, but she preferred obscurity. She didn't want anyone to see her, or recognize her, not when she'd once been Manhattan Ballet's principal ballerina, loved and adored for her grace, talent, and beauty.

Ava's life consisted of work and the ballet. Just as it had always been work, and the ballet, although before she'd been on the stage, not in the back row of seats in the auditorium.

He knew her routine because he had her followed. The security detail was discreet and she never even knew they were there, just as she didn't know the town car was his, and the driver his, too. She didn't know the Manhattan Ballet had initially given her the first part-time teaching job because he'd insisted the company arrange something for her—or he'd pull his support. The company listened. He was their largest benefactor, after all.

She didn't know he'd been in the background opening doors, smoothing the way for her return, and he didn't want her to know.

It was enough that she was working, and that she'd been promoted several times from a part-time, assistant teacher for the children in the dance school, to working with the older students and the professional dancers in the corp.

Malcolm McKenzie didn't mind the money. It wasn't that much, considering. Not when one was looking at the long-term, and he was looking at the long-term. Ava was his wife and the mother of his son.

The only problem was that while she remembered young Jack, Ava didn't remember marrying Malcolm.

Chapter Two

I T WAS COLD and the cold made her hurt even more than she normally did, which meant she moved even more slowly.

Ava smiled gratefully at her doorman as he patiently held the apartment building's front door open for her. He was such a nice man, so patient, too. "Thank you, Robert," she said, aware that she was moving like an old woman, feet inching along, more like a shuffle than a walk. The cold made her stiff, and the stiffness knocked her off balance. If she had the energy, she'd go back upstairs and get her cane. This was one of those days when she could have used the support.

"Need a hand, Ms. Galvan?" Robert asked, obviously concerned by her limping progress. It was the progress of a snail. She was certain it was painful to watch.

She flashed the doorman a small, fierce smile, wanting to put him at ease. How could she complain to him when he stood for hours in the bitter weather?

"No, I'm good. I've got this," she answered, glancing at the pavement in front of her, checking for ice. It'd only take one misstep and today she'd go crashing down and then she'd really hurt.

"Sure you don't want me to lend you an arm—"

"No, Robert. I'm twenty-nine, not eighty-nine."

He laughed, as she'd intended. "Very good, Ms. Galvan. You have a good day."

"You, too." She focused her attention on the black sedan parked at the curb waiting for her. *Put one foot in front of the other*, she sang in her head, teeth gritted against the pain, *and soon you'll be walking out the door....*

She blinked back tears as she sang the line again. Oh, she hurt. Hurt bad today. Where was that cane? Why had she thought she'd manage without it? Ava hadn't wanted to leave bed today. Hadn't wanted to shower and get dressed and come downstairs to travel across town to the Manhattan Ballet Company and School, located on Eighth and Forty-Eighth

But she had forced herself up. And she forced herself to shower and dress and now she was here, almost to the car. She had to get up and go to work, because it was all she had now. She couldn't let the cold, or her stiffness stop her. She needed the Manhattan Ballet.

Her driver, Mickey Fitzgerald, moved towards her and took her elbow. "Mind the ice in front of you," he said.

"You and Robert are like little old ladies fussing, always

over me," she scolded, even as she leaned on his arm, secretly thankful for Mickey's support.

"Now those are fighting words, Ms. Galvan, and you don't want to fight Mickey Fitzgerald. I'm a former featherweight champion—"

"Yes, and not just Irish, but world." She smiled up at him. "How could I forget that the great Mickey Fitzgerald is my very own chauffeur, shuttling me to and from work every day?"

"I am thinking I hear a little disrespect," he said, shifting his grip to keep her supported as she bent her knees to slide into the back of the town car.

She winced as she brought her legs into the car, one by one. "No disrespect," she said, drawing a ragged breath. "You know I love you too much for that."

"Hmph!" His gruffness couldn't hide his fierce protective streak, though.

Mickey treated her like a princess. Ava didn't know how she'd lucked out, finding a driver as kind and good as Mickey Fitzgerald. He closed the door behind her and went around to the driver side.

As he got behind the wheel, he glanced at her in the rearview mirror. "It's a cold one, though, isn't it?"

"It is," she agreed, glancing up at the steel gray sky.

Snow was expected late tonight. The storm was supposed to dump seven to eight inches, possibly more. If that happened, the city would shut down. She prayed that wasn't the case. It was miserable being trapped in her apartment.

"This would have been a good day for your cane," he added, shifting into drive, and merging effortlessly with traffic.

"Or my walker."

"Or your walker," he agreed. He shot her another glance in the rear view mirror. "But you're too proud, aren't you?"

She rolled her eyes. "People treat me differently when I use them."

"You are different. You're special. Don't forget that."

She smiled faintly, but his words gave her a pang. She'd once believed she was special. It was what made her leave Buenos Aires as a young teenager to train in New York City. She left her family and friends to be a ballerina. She'd given up everything for dance…

Buenos Aires. It'd be hot there now. Summer. She should go back. Warm up.

But it wouldn't happen. She'd never go back, not like this. It would be too difficult traveling. She'd need too much help, and she didn't like help. Didn't like being dependent on anyone for anything, Even though she was terribly dependent at the same time.

She hadn't always been.

She'd once been so independent that she'd left Argentina at thirteen. She'd been so focused, so determined. She was going to be a great dancer. And she'd come close. She'd been made a soloist with the Manhattan Ballet at the age of twenty-one, and by twenty-three was one of their youngest principals.

She'd loved it. Loved the work, the discipline, the passion. And the fame. She'd been someone important—

Ava exhaled slowly, deeply.

But that was a long time ago, too. A different lifetime. Better to not remember. Easier to accept who she was today if she didn't let herself remember who she had once been.

MALCOLM WAS IN a meeting with his corporation's chief financial officer when he got a text from Mickey Fitzgerald.

She's not moving well today. Thought you would want to know.

Colm read the message and put away his phone but he thought about Mickey's text quite a few times during the rest of the meeting. Mickey didn't often send updates, but the fact that he had sent one today, concerned Colm.

If Mickey was worried about Ava, Colm was, too.

Obviously, it was time to pay Ava a call.

AVA WAS IN the hallway of the second floor, observing one of the younger classes at the barre through the glass on the door. Her next class wouldn't start for another half hour, but she loved watching the children in class and rehearsal. They were so innocent and eager. So hopeful, too. The very young ones made her feel protective, and yes, wistful. Not every little girl falls in love with ballet, but those who do, fall hard.

To dance is to dream. *You must believe you can float...fly. To soar requires dedication, discipline, training.* The five and six year olds were just starting with their training, each class beginning with the barre work.

Ava felt herself breathe and exhale, her own leg muscles tightening, lengthening with each of the children's battement tendu.

The barre work wasn't just about training the body, but also training the mind.

At the barre, you'd quiet your mind and become focused, attentive to each stretch, bend, extension, adjusting to each correction. These very young girls were just learning the craft, but the learning would never end. A dancer's goal was perfection. A lifelong quest, made even more difficult as one aged, and battled time and injuries.

Standing at the glass, for a moment, Ava was one of them, all air and grace and strength, and then suddenly she felt a prickle at the back of her neck and an odd sensation in her belly. She wasn't alone anymore. Someone else was here, watching her.

She turned away from the door, leaving one hand on the wood for balance, and looked behind her. For a split second there was no one there. Just the quiet hall leading to the stairs. And yet her skin continued to prickle and tingle.

And then she saw him, standing in the stairwell. Malcolm.

Her legs almost went out.

It'd been a year since she'd last seen him. A year of wondering if she'd ever see him again and now he was here.

Malcolm stepped from the stairwell and walked towards her. "Hello, Ava."

She'd heard his voice so many nights in her sleep, and yet in the quiet hallway, it was deeper, rougher than she remembered. She flushed, going hot, then cold. She reached for the door, gripping the knob for strength. "You scared me."

"I'm sorry."

He sounded sincere. Concerned. But if her memory—the limited memory she had—was true, he'd never been a sweet or sensitive man. He was brilliant, intense, successful, charismatic. But gentle? Sensitive? Never.

"What brings you to the school?" she asked, hearing the tremor in her voice and hating it.

"I was looking for you."

"You knew I was here?"

He nodded. "I've kept tabs on you."

"Why?"

"I wanted to be sure you were safe."

She struggled to smile. "I'm fine. See?" And yet her legs weren't steady and she was leaning now against the door, afraid that any second she'd go down. She wished she'd brought her cane. Wished—

And just like that, he was at her side, wrapping an arm around her waist. "I've got you," he said. "You're okay."

It was hard to think clearly with him there at her side.

Her skin burned where he touched her. She felt waves of heat rush through her. At that moment, she felt anything but okay. "I'd like to sit down."

"Where?"

"There's an empty studio next door. I'm sure there's a chair inside."

He supported her as they walked down the hall to the large room lined with floor to ceiling mirrors on one wall and barres on the opposite. An upright piano was in one corner and a chair in another.

She sank gratefully down in the chair. He stepped away, giving her distance.

"I'm shocked," she said, struggling to smile and failing miserably.

"Why? You know I've been waiting to hear from you. I was sure I'd hear from you before Christmas, certain you'd be with us for Christmas—"

"Malcolm—"

"How was your Christmas?"

Her eyes stung. Her chest ached. It had been a very quiet Christmas. No tree. No decorations. No parties or festive meals. A few of her students had given her gifts, trinkets and tokens of their affection, and yet somehow it had only made her lonelier. "It was fine."

"Did you go anywhere? Make it a proper holiday?"

A lump filled her throat. "No, I spent it at home."

"You were happy, though?"

Everything inside her hurt. Was she happy? No. But she was determined to learn to be happy. Determined to continue piecing her life back together. But it wasn't a smooth process. There were many fits and starts, as well as unexpected setbacks. Like a fall on an icy curb. The relentless ache in her bones when buffeted by the frigid wind. "I'm healthy," she said with a faint smile. "That's something."

His harsh expression eased somewhat. "Yes, it is." He hesitated, his gaze scrutinizing her, moving from head to toe. "I did hope to hear from you. I'd hoped you'd join us for the holidays."

"Malcolm, we talked about this last time."

"Last *year*. And much has changed in the past year."

Fear made her heart race. "*I* haven't changed."

His cool blue-green gaze held hers, challenging her. "I think you have."

"*No*!" The denial burst from her, desperation sharpening her voice. "You're not a doctor. A psychiatrist. Or a therapist. You're not an expert. We have no reason to question the decision made—"

"But we do. We have our son."

It was like tearing a scab from a wound. He couldn't possibly think they could go back and undo all that had been done. *Humpty Dumpty sat on the wall…Humpty Dumpty took a big fall…*

"Don't," she whispered, lifting a hand as if she could hold him back.

The room swirled, her head spinning. Ava gulped in breaths, fighting the dizziness. If she thought she could, she'd leave the chair, race from the room, but her legs were shaking and her pulse was racing and it was all she could manage just to sit upright in the chair.

"He deserves better," Malcolm continued, his tone quiet, and yet flat, firm. "He deserves more. More from you...me...us."

"I terrified him last time. He hated me—"

"He was two. He was shy and, yes, scared, but he would have overcome his fear if you'd given him the opportunity."

"That's not what you said then!"

"I said he needed time. I didn't want you to leave."

But you let me go, she thought, *and you were glad to see me go*. "That's not true," she said after a moment. "You're not happy when I'm there...with you. It stresses you. I feel it, and your disappointment. I hate your disappointment. It's upsetting, and when I get emotional you know I can't think clearly. I can't remember things properly. Everything just falls apart."

"You had a traumatic brain injury. The healing process is long—"

"Which annoys you."

"What annoys me is that you are making assumptions, and, frankly, they're not true. Your mind is stronger. Your memory is better. Will you always have issues? Yes. But I accept that, and I accept that there are limitations, and I'm prepared to work through and around the limitations. But I need your help. I need you to work with us, too."

Her eyes burned and she blinked. "But aren't you the man that demands perfection?"

"That's nonsense." Colm stood over her, his body big, broad, muscular, his hands knotted at his sides. He'd always had broad shoulders and long legs, but he was leaner now than she'd remembered, and with his dark blonde hair cropped close, his jaw and cheekbones jutted, hard, and uncompromising.

Malcolm McKenzie's father was Scottish, his mother American and he'd been raised for the first thirteen and a half years of his life running wild in the Highlands, before being sent to boarding school in England for high school. Eton was an elite school, arguably the best boys senior school in the United Kingdom, but Malcolm had hated it. He didn't want to board. He longed to be a day student, back home with his family and the freedom he craved. But during his second year at Eton his parents divorced and his father remarried and his mother, an American by birth, returned to New York.

The childhood he knew was gone. His father had a new young bride and they quickly filled the old manor house with young half brothers and sisters. It only took a couple visits home to realize he'd become redundant. He wasn't needed home anymore. In fact, he was expected to get on with his life—university, work, independence. And so he did just that, with ruthless determination.

When Ava first met him, she'd heard him referred to as a modern day Celtic warrior. A raider. He took what he wanted without regard to the feelings, or needs, of others.

Ava had been intrigued despite his reputation. She'd wanted to know him, wanting to know the real Malcolm McKenzie.

She'd liked who she'd discovered. Yes, he was tough. He was a man that took no prisoners and refused to compromise, but his impossible ideals resonated with her.

"Is it?" She tipped her head back, meeting his cool blue-green gaze. "Your entire life has been a quest for perfection, and now you propose to saddle yourself with me? A woman who can't always remember her own address?"

He dropped suddenly to his haunches, squatting before her, his hands going to her knees. "That man may have once existed, Ava, but he died the night you were injured. He's gone. He's been gone for nearly four years. But you are here, alive, and we need you, with us. Our family is incomplete without you."

She closed her eyes, trying to shut out his words and voice, as well as the set of his mouth and hard beauty of his features. And yet, with her eyes closed, all she could feel was the heat and pressure of his hands on her knees. His skin was so warm that it burned her.

"I refuse to allow you to give up on us, and our son," he added fiercely. "You and I created him. He is ours, and he needs you, his mother. It's time you came home and became that mother."

She squeezed her eyes more tightly closed. My God, did Colm know what he was doing? Did he understand how devastating, not to mention dangerous, this could be for all of them? "Last year, last December, you felt differently. You said Jack was better off without me."

"I said *maybe*."

She opened her eyes, looked into his, holding his gaze. "But they were your words, Colm. You had doubts, serious doubts, about my ability to properly care for Jack."

"I spoke in a moment of anger and frustration. I regret those words—"

"I remember those words." How could she not? She wrote them down in her little journal. She wrote them down and reread them daily so that she wouldn't forget why she was alone. So that she wouldn't forget why she didn't see her son.

She'd hurt Jack, a year ago December. She'd lost him. No, *left* him.

She'd left a two year old in a busy shopping center. Worse, she hadn't even realized that she'd left Jack. She hadn't even remembered that she'd had a son. She'd gotten distracted by something and in that distracted moment her memory failed her, and she'd simply walked out of the mall and had kept walking. She walked until she was lost, panicked, pathetically confused. She only remembered those details because she'd written them down that night after the police found her and reunited her with Colm and Jack. She'd written down everything she'd been told so that she'd understand that while such a mistake could be forgiven, it couldn't be forgotten.

Rereading that day's journal entry horrified her every time. Jack could have died. She could have died. The outing could have ended tragically. Thank God it didn't. But the police and social services were right. She wasn't fit to be a mother. Malcolm had been irresponsible to trust her with a toddler. She'd failed Malcolm and their son. And she'd learned her lesson. They'd all learned their lesson.

This is why she lived in New York, and this is why her child lived with his father in Florida, and this is why dance was everything. It's all she had.

It's all she'd ever have. She couldn't be trusted. Her mind was a dangerous thing.

"You and I both know it would be a mistake for me to return," she said softly, hoarsely, even as the studio door opened and young girls in pink tights and black leotards filed in.

Ava attempted to rise. Without her cane she was hopeless. Colm took her elbow, drawing her up. "Jack's older now, and you're stronger," he said flatly. "The fact that you are here, teaching four classes a day, proves you've made huge strides. If you can teach the professional dancers, as well as take care of these children, you can certainly take care of our son."

"You don't know that."

He was standing so close that she could feel his intense energy slam into her, wave after wave of shimmering heat and strength.

"I know we have to try."

Something in his tone made her look up and their eyes locked. Determination shone in his eyes. He was serious. Her tummy flipped, her mouth dried. "You need to let me go. It's time you moved on."

His gaze never wavered. Fire burned in the blue-green depths. "You don't mean that."

She licked her upper lip, wetting the painfully dry skin. "I do." She swallowed hard, looked away, noting the children taking position at the barre, and the pianist taking her seat at the upright piano in the corner. "I'm not trying to be rude, either. But I have to teach now. I have to focus on my class. I'm their teacher—"

"And Jack's mother."

She flinched. "I can't talk about it anymore. I need to gather my thoughts. Review my notes. I can't teach without my notes."

"I'll leave so that you can teach, but I'll be back end of the day, and we're going to talk—"

"We have nothing to discuss."

"That's not true, and you know it. I'll be back when you're finished and we'll sit, and eat, and we're going to talk about the steps we need to take to bring you home—"

"It's not my home!"

"Yes, it is," he interrupted tautly. "But you're just too scared to admit it." And then he was gone, walking out of the studio, moving swiftly, without a glance back.

Chapter Three

YES, HE WAS right. She was scared. She was terrified. And she had every right to be terrified. She was not the same person she used to be. She would never be the same person and he didn't have to wake up in a strange body with a strange brain every day and wonder who he was, and where he was, and then struggle to piece together a life that had massive gaps because he'd lost huge chunks of his memory—memories that would probably never come back.

Thank God, she remembered music and language. And while she couldn't dance anymore—her balance and coordination were shot—she remembered her classical training, and could teach.

But she battled through every day. Nothing was easy or familiar and her entire goal was to just get by.

To try to fit in.

To try to be normal.

Even though she had no idea what normal was anymore.

After Colm left, Ava struggled to get through her two

remaining afternoon classes. It took every bit of her focus and energy to stay on task, and today she was forced to rely heavily on her notebook for teaching the classes.

The notebook was her lifeline. After losing Jack that day fourteen months ago, Ava began meeting with therapists again on memory strategies, and the specialist had recommended that Ava write everything down, and organize herself with a planner, and making lists and breaking action items down into steps. But then the key was to refer to those notes, again and again, modifying her lists, making new lists, honoring the first rule of memory—write everything down in one spot (her notebook). And then the second rule of memory—write it down while it's fresh in her mind.

She'd learned through trial and error to write more, not less. She needed complete notes, detailed notes, so that she understood what she was trying to tell herself.

The notes helped, too. They allowed her to function, and accomplish more. But she lived in fear of the day she lost her notebook. Would she remember what she needed to remember, without it?

Would she remember the last year if the book of memories disappeared?

As her last class for the day filed out, Ava spotted a shadow in the doorway.

Malcolm. He was back.

Just seeing his powerful frame in the doorway made her tremble. She wasn't afraid of him, but of how she felt when near him. They'd had such a physical relationship. They'd connected through skin and sex and funny how she could forget words and names and places she was supposed to go, but she could still remember him. She could still remember how they'd been once. She no longer loved him, and her memories since the accident were patchy at best, but her body had never had a problem recognizing him.

And, as he crossed the room towards her, she felt the old thrill ripple through her. It was impossible to look at him without feeling a throb of awe, and desire. He moved like a great athlete, with leashed strength, and power, and grace. She responded to him the way she responded to music and dance…instinctively.

"I'd rather hoped you wouldn't return," she said.

"Not surprised. I was a bit of an ass earlier. I'm sorry."

She shot him a swift glance, surprised. He was smiling faintly, firm lips quirked, eyes crinkling at the corners.

She didn't know this Malcolm. At least, she didn't remember this Malcolm. "I know I have memory issues, but I don't remember you apologizing very often."

The corner of his mouth lifted higher. "In this case, your memory serves you well."

Ava felt a pang, her chest tightening with emotion. "How do you do that?" she whispered. "How do you still make me feel so much?"

"That's just how we've always been."

"But even after a year?"

"We're supposed to be together, Ava. But I have a feeling you don't write that down in your notebook. I have a feeling you write anything but that down."

He knew her so well that it scared her. She looked away, out the window. It was dark out. It looked cold.

"You have me at a disadvantage," she said after a moment, glancing back at him. "You can remember things without needing to write them down. Both good and bad. You can go through your memories and analyze them. I have nothing to analyze."

"And yet you try. You record facts and details and pour over them."

"Yes." Her gaze met his, and she felt a jolt of awareness, and appreciation. He was so impossibly good-looking. By far, the most handsome man she'd ever met. And he'd once been hers.

"Maybe that's the mistake," he said. "Maybe you need to think less, and feel more."

"Then I'd feel absolute panic because I'd realize what a disaster I am—" She broke off and swallowed hard. Her eyes burned and her chest felt impossibly tender. "I don't think you understand, Colm, how hard every little thing is for me. Nothing comes easy. Everything requires so much effort."

"Because you try to do everything on your own. Let us help you, Ava. Let us make it easier. We can."

"I wish I could believe you."

"What if I could prove it to you?"

Her gaze locked with his. "How would you do that?"

"Come away with me for the weekend. It's going to snow tonight—hard—the city will be shut down tomorrow, and probably the day after. So let's make it a long weekend. Let's escape the cold and play and have fun."

Play. Have fun. Now those were foreign concepts. "I don't think I know how to do that."

"I know. But I can show you." And then he smiled at her, and there was heat in his eyes and she couldn't help but respond, a shiver of pleasure racing through her.

"You are far too attractive, you know," she said huskily.

His smile deepened. His blue-green eyes glinted. "We used to have fun together, Ava. Let's have fun again."

"What would we do?"

"Soak up the sun. Eat good food. Listen to music. Cruise around the island."

Her eyebrows lifted. "The island?"

"I bought a little place in the Caribbean. It's gorgeous there right now. Not too hot. Not at all humid. It's pretty perfect."

She thought of her small apartment and how tonight's big snow storm would trap her inside as she was unable to navigate the snow and ice on her own. "It does sound nice."

"So come with me. Have fun with me."

It was tempting, so tempting. Her gaze searched his. "I can't just leave here…drop everything…"

"The city is going to shut down. The school will close.

The professional dancers might stagger in for a class, but they don't need you. So think about what you need…the sun, the sea, some R&R." He smiled at her, teasing, coaxing. "Doesn't that sound appealing?"

"Very."

"So give yourself permission to unplug for a few days. You've earned the break. I'm sure you haven't taken any vacation time in the past year."

"I haven't."

"So take a little vacation now. Let the sun warm you up and get that ache out of your bones."

She chewed on the inside of her lip, tempted, so very tempted, because she did hurt. All the time. And she was exhausted from trying so hard to stay on top of things, and organized. She couldn't even remember what a holiday felt like.

Her gaze met his, and held. "Why are you doing this? Why go to all this trouble for me?"

For a moment he just stared at her and then his hard features gentled. "That's easy," he said gruffly. "I want to spend time with you. I've missed you."

Chapter Four

*H*E MISSED HER.

Malcolm McKenzie, the Scottish-American tycoon who'd made his fortune off real estate, internet startups, and shrewd investments, missed *her*.

"You could have any woman," she said, struggling to smile, wanting to be playful, but her heart hurt.

She wasn't right for him, not anymore. He and Jack both deserved better. More.

"Yes, I could, and I want you." He lifted a hand. "And don't ask why. I'm not going to do that now, standing here, when you're clearly dead on your feet. We will have all the time in the world once we get to the house on St. Barts. So, let's get your things and go to the car before the storm starts and keeps us from flying out tonight."

He helped her gather her black cashmere shawl and her notebook and pen. Together, they walked to her small office where she retrieved her winter coat, hat, and gloves. They rode, silent, down to the lobby in the elevator. Ava glanced at Colm's profile as he opened the building's front door and they were greeted by an icy blast of air.

Colm looked big and fierce and forbidding.

What was she doing, agreeing to go away with him?

Why was she agreeing to his?

As they left the building, she shivered, and wobbled, and wished yet again she'd brought her cane today.

Colm wrapped an arm around her waist, steadying her. "You're doing great," he said.

She was wearing the thickest of coats but the pressure of his arm, the touch at her waist made her gulp for air. "I'm okay," she protested. "I'm not going to fall."

"Not taking any chances."

She shot him a swift glance. "I manage just fine when you're not around."

He arched a brow, but didn't contradict her.

She spotted the town car at the curb. Mickey was standing by the black sedan, waiting for her. "My car's here," she said. "Do you have one, too?"

"No. I figured we could use your car."

Frowning, she glanced up at him. "Mickey might have plans."

Colm shrugged. "He might, and then he might not. Let's ask him."

Malcolm did just that, asking if Mickey could drive them to Teterboro, the executive airport that served metropolitan New York. The airport was just across the Hudson in New

Jersey. Mickey knew where it was.

"Not a problem. I can take you and Ms. Galvan wherever you want to go," the driver answered.

"Good. My plane's ready. We just need to get there."

In the back of the car, Ava glanced at Colm. "You were so very sure of me, weren't you?

"I wasn't sure of you. Just hopeful." His mouth curved. "And then there's the fact that I have confidence in my negotiation skills. I've been told I can be persuasive."

"Sounds like something I might have said," she muttered grumpily.

"Indeed."

Mickey shifted into drive, putting the car in motion, and seconds later they'd merged into the evening traffic. A horn blared behind them but, but neither Ava nor Malcolm paid the honking cars and taxis any attention.

After a moment, Colm asked her about the new ballet premiering in February, just before Valentine's Day. Ava shared that it was a love story set during WWII, and since it was part of the Holocaust, it was tragic, but the ending was powerful and redemptive. She loved the choreography and music and was looking forward to it staged.

Colm kept asking questions and she talked, relaxing as she focused on the thing she knew best—dance.

But that ease vanished thirty minutes later when they pulled up to the executive terminal.

Ava stiffened as she spotted the airport's tower and then

saw the sleek, white jets dotting on the tarmac.

What on earth was she doing? How could she have agreed to Colm's plan? Fear swamped her, clouding her thoughts, making her head spin.

She couldn't leave the car. Couldn't leave Mickey. This was a mistake, she thought. She couldn't go to St. Barts.

She should be home right now. She needed to keep her routine. Bad things always happened when she changed her schedule, or did things differently. "No. I can't do this," she said, drawing back from the door as Mickey came around to open it for them. "It's not a good idea."

"There's no reason to panic—"

"There's every reason in the world! When I change things, do things differently, everything falls apart. I fall apart. I don't want that to happen, and neither do you."

"You're not getting rid of me, Ava."

"I know what Jack needs, and it's not me."

"What about me?" he demanded, his voice low, terse. "Are you going to speak for my needs as well?"

She stared up into his face, searching his eyes. "I know—"

"Ava, you don't know. And while I love that you have a mind of your own, and a fierce desire to be independent, in this instance, you are wrong." His voice dropped, deepening. "I've tried to be patient. I've tried to let you do things at your pace, but my patience is gone. It's time to do what I think is right, for you, for Jack, and for me."

"Which means?"

"That we're going to figure us out. Once and for all."

He scooped her into his arms, stepped from the car, and carried her past Mickey, to walk the short distance from the car to the parked jet. The first snowflakes were falling in dizzying whirl of white.

"Put me down!" Ava demanded, pressing against Colm's thick shoulders and then giving him a shove in the middle of his chest. Snowflakes were sticking to his jacket and dusting their heads. She supposed it was cold but she was too upset to feel it.

Malcolm ignored her, crossing the tarmac in long, determined strides.

Ava glanced back at Mickey who was standing next to the car, arms folded, looking very much like a sentry, except he shouldn't be standing there frozen. He should be coming to her assistance. "Mickey, help me!" she cried, pounding on Colm's chest again. "Don't let him take me. You can't let him do this—"

"Stop shouting," Colm cut her short her. "He's not going to help you. Mickey works for me. He's always worked for me. Everything you have has been provided by me. Your apartment, your job, your security detail—"

"My security detail?"

"Yes. Your security detail. Robert, your doorman. Mickey, your driver. Peter at the Ballet—"

"Peter, the custodian?"

"He's not a janitor. He's a retired Secret Service agent,

and he's there to protect you. So stop shouting and flinging yourself around before you get hurt."

Her jaw dropped. Her expression was one of shock. "*You* hired all of those people?"

"Screened them. Hired them. Monitored them." He shifted her weight in the arms and mounted the stairs, climbing the folding stairs quickly, effortlessly.

"Why?"

"To keep you safe, dammit!"

She stared at him, appalled. "You are out of your mind."

"Maybe," he admitted grimly as the crew closed the jet door, securing it. He nodded to the pilots and then the male flight steward even as her put her down in one of the oversized leather chairs in the main galley. "Buckle up," he said. "We want to get out of here quickly. Conditions are worsening. If we're going to take off tonight, we need to do it now."

"I've changed my mind. I don't want to go." She tried to stand.

He pushed her back down. "You want to go. You're just being stubborn."

"Now you're making me angry," she snapped as he reached across her lap to buckle the seatbelt.

"And you're being difficult." He dropped into the seat across from hers and buckled his belt. "We're here. We're going. End of discussion."

She leaned towards him, spitting mad. "This is why we're not together! You're arrogant, and controlling, and overpowering—"

"That's not why we're not together. We're not together because we had a spat in Palm Beach a year ago and you ran away."

"It wasn't a spat! It was a catastrophe. And you said as much."

"I said things I regret," he agreed. "But I've apologized too many times to count."

"So maybe you should take the hint and leave me alone."

"I refuse to give up on us."

"It's pathetic."

He shot her a dark, fierce look. "Maybe it's time we stopped talking and just enjoyed the flight."

FOR THE NEXT thirty minutes all was quiet. Colm was sitting with his head tipped back and his eyes closed. Ava stared out the window until she couldn't stand it any longer and then turned to focus on Malcolm.

Eventually, he sighed, and without opening his eyes, said, "Jack does the same thing. But he's three, not twenty-nine."

"What are you talking about?"

"The staring thing. It's his favorite game when I'm working."

"I'm so mad at you."

"For taking you on a Caribbean holiday when Manhattan is going to be buried under a foot of snow and ice?"

"That's not the point and you know it. And even if I'd wanted to go with you—"

"You did agree, initially."

"Initially." She stressed. "And then I changed my mind. And even if I hadn't changed my mind, you didn't even let me pack anything. I've no suitcase. I don't have any clothes."

"There are clothes for you at the villa."

"Whose clothes?"

"Yours." He finally opened his eyes, looked at her. "I ordered them for you thinking you'd be with us this Christmas."

He'd hoped she'd be there with them for Christmas? A pang shot through her and for a moment she couldn't breathe. The sharp emotion made her thoughts scatter. It took her a moment to focus. "Don't try to make me feel guilty."

"You can feel guilty if you want. I'm just stating facts."

Facts. Details. It was a good reminder. She needed to make some notes, write down what was happening, and why. But she couldn't find the notebook on her, and she patted her coat that she'd draped across her legs but couldn't find it there.

She turned the coat inside out to check the coat's lavender silk interior, feeling for the hidden pockets.

"What are you looking for?" Colm asked after a moment.

"My notebook." She lifted the wool coat, shook it hard, and checked the outside pockets once more. "I could have sworn I put the notebook in this pocket when we were leaving the school. I always put it in this pocket." She looked at him, trying not to panic but worried. She couldn't imagine getting through a day without the notebook much less a long weekend. "I need it. I use it for everything."

"We can get you a new one."

"I don't want a new one. I need my book. It has all my information in it. Plans, calendar, descriptions and directions…how to do things…when to do things."

"I can see why you'd want it in Manhattan, but we're going to be on holiday. Can you not survive without it for a few days?"

She bit her lip, glanced to the window, but could see nothing but darkness beyond the glass. "I just don't know where I dropped it. I don't know if it's in Mickey's car or—" She broke off as she turned towards him. "And that reminds me, you deceived me. You've been deceiving me for months…maybe even years. Mickey wasn't my driver. He was yours. He worked for you."

"Yes."

"And Robert, my doorman. How is it you could hire him?"

"It's my building, so I have a say in who works there."

Your building, she silently repeated, staring at him, torn between shock, awe and horror. Maybe what she felt was a little of all three. "Your building. Your doorman. Your driver. And the job at the ballet? Was that yours, too?"

"Yes. No."

"Which is it?"

"I asked them to put together a position for you, but the promotions and increased hours and responsibilities, that was all you."

"But who paid for my salary, and each of the increases that came with the promotions? From the ballet company? Or from you, funneling it to the company?"

He didn't say anything but that was answer enough. She knotted her hands in her lap, fingers locking tight. She was heartsick. Embarrassed. All this time she'd felt so independent. She'd thought she was accomplishing something, doing something…

But she wasn't independent. She was the exact opposite. She was a joke. He'd turned her into a joke—

"Why do you do that to yourself?" he asked, his voice deep, rough. "I know what you're doing. You're beating yourself up. Torturing yourself."

"I left Argentina as a thirteen-year-old because I had a dream for myself, and I was determined to be successful and independent. And after I was hurt, I was again determined to be independent, and I thought I was. Only now I discover everything I thought I achieved is fake. You pulled all these strings and orchestrated all the events so that it would seem like I was successful—"

"That's not how it was," he interrupted harshly.

"No?" Her voice cracked and she struggled with her

composure. "Because it sure looks that way. It seems I must be hopelessly damaged if my former lover must create an elaborate charade to give me a sense of purpose and identity—"

"Stop it. You're twisting things, making my support into something ugly."

"If it's not ugly, what it is? What do you call your manipulation?"

"Concern. Love. Protection."

"Love doesn't hide and deceive. But that's what you've been doing with me." Her voice broke again, and this time she couldn't continue, not when she was battling back the tears. She pressed her nails to the tops of her thighs, determined not to cry. Emotion wasn't her friend. She couldn't let herself lose it.

"You wanted to return to work, but you weren't strong enough to get to and from the school and theater, so I made sure you could go, and not tire yourself. And I don't regret it. I'm glad I did it, and I'd do it all over again because you needed someone to help you, someone to take care of you—"

"Yet you let me believe I'd earned the job and found the apartment." Her gaze locked with his. "You let me believe I was coping with life again."

"Because you are. You have been. You are clearly healing. If you weren't better, I wouldn't be pushing for you to come home."

"Your home is not my home, Malcolm. Your home has

never been my home. To be honest, I don't know why we're even here, doing this."

He arched a brow. "I know you have memory issues, but Ava, is it that easy to forget you have a son?"

She ground her teeth together. "And I hurt him. I remember that, too."

"You have forgotten so many things. Why can't you let yourself forget that one day?"

"Because I can't afford to forget that I abandoned a two-year-old. I walked away from him without a second thought, and thank God nothing tragic happened that day, but it could have."

Colm said nothing for a long moment, his lashes lowered, gaze narrowed as he studied her. And then he shook his head. "You're wrong, Ava. Something tragic did happen that day. We lost you, Jack and I. And this time it sounds like you're not coming back."

Chapter Five

COLM WATCHED AS she swiftly averted her head, her teeth sinking into her lush lower lip. From the back of her head with the tightly pinned chignon, he couldn't tell if she was fighting tears or angry words, but either way, he didn't care.

He was so frustrated right now.

He was so frustrated with the doctors and the therapists and all the experts who told him to give her space. Let her heal in her time. They'd said she'd need to grieve the loss of her old self as she came to terms with her new self.

But they'd never said she'd walk away from them.

They'd never said she'd give up.

What happened to her fire? Her conviction? Where was her backbone?

Ava Galvan was the strongest, most passionate woman he'd ever known. She was fierce and funny and so very loving. He understood she'd been hurt—terribly, terribly hurt—but she was making huge strides in her recovery and then that day in Florida had turned it inside out.

Turned all of them inside out.

"What has happened to you?" he demanded lowly. "Where's your courage? Your fire? Where is the Ava I know? You aren't a quitter and yet you've quit. You've quit on all of us—"

"I was *hurt*." Her head jerked up and her dark gaze clashed with his. "I would think you'd remember. Your memory is supposed to be intact."

"Yes, it is, and I remember how even after the accident you wanted to dance again and live again and love again but that's all gone. You're a shell of yourself, and brittle as hell."

She jerked her chin higher even as her dark eyes turned liquid. "I'm sorry I can't be the woman you want me to be. But there was an accident. I was hurt. End of story."

But that wasn't the end of story, he thought, barely hanging onto his temper. It wasn't close to end of story. He didn't want to be angry with her. God knows, the accident hadn't been her fault. She'd suffered, terribly. He'd vowed to stick by her side and he had, until the doctors demanded that Colm step back and give Ava space. They'd said he was starting to do more harm than good by pushing her so much. The doctors thought she needed peace and quiet…a chance to heal.

And so he'd backed away during the first year of her rehabilitation, focusing on the baby, but when she'd reached out to him at the end of a year, he turned his world upside down to accommodate Ava. He bought a house in Palm Beach that was all one level so she wouldn't have to deal with stairs. He'd turned one of the garages into a special gym so she could continue her rehab work. For a year, they tried to make it work, and he'd been hopeful that she was doing better, but it was always a struggle for her. She would get upset and her tears frightened Jack. Sometimes she'd look at Jack and not know what to say or do, treating him as if he were a stranger, but still, Colm hoped.

He refused to give up on her, and to show his commitment, he married her. It had been a small private service at Thanksgiving, just the three of them, plus the necessary witnesses, and he'd married her to cement their relationship.

Ten days later, Ava took Jack out and walked away from him, and just kept walking.

She was found five miles from the shopping center, lost, disoriented, unable to provide the police any information. For twelve hours she didn't even remember her name, and then when she did remember, she wasn't Ava McKenzie, but Ava Galvan.

She didn't remember marrying Colm. Didn't remember taking Jack out. Didn't remember the year in Palm Beach at all.

In her mind, she was still living in New York. Still hoping to return to the ballet.

And so he did what the doctors and specialists told him to do. He let her return to New York, and the ballet, and the life she wanted.

But, all the while, he was raising a little boy who didn't understand where his mother had gone, and Colm didn't know how to put all the pieces together.

What was the right thing to do? What was the smart thing to do?

He didn't even know if he loved Ava anymore. But he still felt responsible for her. He was loyal. He was determined to do what he had to do. It's how he was raised. It was who he was.

But it was confusing. For all of them.

"It's not too late to tell your flight crew to turn the plane around," she said softly. Her gaze met his and her expression was painfully grave. "We could probably still land in Teterboro."

For a moment, he didn't speak, too busy trying to process his wildly conflicting feelings. He wanted her. He didn't want her. He missed her. He was exhausted by the struggle to get close to her. He'd never give up on her. He didn't know if he should give up on her.

Just looking at her, he felt connected to her. When near her, he knew they were still meant to be together.

But if she didn't feel it? If she didn't believe it?

Was it time to let her go? Or was it time to break through this wall and reserve she'd constructed around her following that incident last December?

He didn't know. He needed to know. He needed clarity,

as well as peace.

As if reading his mind, her lips curved sadly. "Someday you have to accept facts."

He stared at her for a long moment, then shrugged. "I'm not there yet."

"But what if I am?"

His chest tightened, a pinch that made him hold his breath and count to ten.

"Then you have to be patient with me," he said lowly. "Because I still want to try."

Emotion flickered in her eyes and her full lips quivered then compressed. She was fighting to hold back tears and it was like a blow to his heart. He clamped his jaw, bottled the emotion tighter.

They'd been through so much.

They'd been through hell and back.

The fight couldn't have been for naught. There had to be hope. A future. A happy ending.

"You're a miracle." His deep voice was pitched so low it was nearly inaudible. "And you need to remember you're a miracle. I do."

Again, her lips quivered and tears filled her beautiful dark eyes. "You're going to make me cry. I don't want to cry."

"Don't cry. You're too pretty to cry," he said, struggling to keep his tone light.

And it was true. She looked like an exquisite butterfly

perched on the butterscotch leather seat across from him—slender, delicate, mysterious.

The accident hadn't marred her beauty. She still turned heads wherever she went. How could you not want to look at her? With her perfect, oval face, full pink lips, high cheekbones, and wide intelligent eyes, she attracted attention and interest.

She shook her head, her expression half-amused, half-exasperated. "Don't try to soften me up with compliments. I might not remember everything but I do remember how charming you can be, and that you're lethal when you want something."

"At least you remember the important things."

She laughed. Good Lord, she laughed.

"You're impossible," she said, her voice throaty, the sound sexy.

And just like that he felt the old jolt, the electric heat that had brought them together, again and again.

"But you like that about me," he drawled, and he saw a flash in her eyes, the laughter chased away by something deeper, hotter.

She felt the heat, too. The physical pull. So the desire wasn't gone. Good to know, he thought, his gaze meeting hers and holding, wanting her to feel what they'd once had. Daring her to let the fire burn again.

HE WAS DOING something to her right now, she thought,

unable to look away from his intense blue-green eyes.

He was challenging her…making her think…feel. So like Colm to throw down the gauntlet, to force her out of safety.

"Impossible," she repeated, her pulse thudding in her veins, her body tingling, a thick hot craving stirring within her.

"You love the impossible." He unfastened his seatbelt and stood.

He was so tall, his shoulders so broad. Her heart jumped, and jumped again as he closed the distance between their leather chairs. "What are you doing?"

"Showing you how much you like the impossible."

"Not smart," she whispered, gulping for air as he leaned over her and unfastened her seat belt.

He drew her up, to her feet. "Now you're just being contrary," he answered, sliding his arms around her and drawing her close against him.

He was oh, so warm, and so very hard. He felt wonderful, too wonderful, and familiar in the kind of way that made her heart ache.

Once, he'd been her man.

Once, he'd been her world.

Colm tilted her chin up, forcing her to look into his eyes. "Remember this," he murmured. "Remember us?"

Her heart was pounding. Her legs went weak.

"We are good together. We fit," he added, his intense eyes held her captive and she stared up at him, thoughts scattering, emotions swirling. She couldn't think straight, didn't know anything right now. "You're not fair." She licked her upper lip, her mouth suddenly dry. "This isn't fair."

"How so?"

She struggled to organize her thoughts, which wasn't easy when her heart was pounding so. He felt so good. He felt like everything she loved. "I think you know I like…this…"

He stroked her cheek. "Mmmm."

It took an effort to speak. Her senses were swimming, nerves screaming with pleasure. "So you're using me….against me."

His lips quirked. "All is fair in love and war."

"Is this war?"

"No, baby, it's love."

But that didn't sound right. It didn't fit. They'd been many things to each other, but he didn't love her. She didn't know why. But love had never been part of the equation.

"It's not love," she said, stiffening, her hands going to his chest to push him back. "I might not remember everything, but I don't think we are—" She broke off, frowned. "It's not love, is it?"

His head dropped, his lips lightly brushing hers. "We've made love a thousand times."

"But that's not love." She leaned back and pressed harder on his firm chest.

He didn't budge. If anything, he held her more firmly,

one of his hands low on her hip, caressing her, stirring her senses, distracting her just when she needed to concentrate most.

His lips trailed a slow path along the side of her neck, making the sensitive skin tingle and burn. "Says who?"

She drew an unsteady breath and closed her eyes as he focused on the soft hollow beneath her ear. Heat flared and everything within her felt bright and taut. She wanted more. She shouldn't want more.

She should put a stop to this. "I can't think when you do that," she murmured, her fingers widening on his chest, feeling the heat of his body, the thudding of his heart.

He was a magnificent male. He was everything she'd ever wanted. But she couldn't want him now. It was hard to remember why. She just knew she couldn't, shouldn't, let this happen.

"You must let me go."

He kissed the line of her jaw. "No."

"You're a barbarian."

He kissed her ever so lightly near the corner of her mouth. "And you love how I can make you feel."

Warmth rushed through her, surging up from her belly through her chest and into her neck and face making her cheeks burn. But she didn't contradict him. She couldn't, not when he was right.

Worse, she wanted him to kiss her, really kiss her. Not these teasing kisses, and pecks, and touches. She wanted his mouth, and his taste. *Him.*

And she was about to tell him what she wanted, her hands sliding up his chest, when the plane shuddered violently in a pocket of turbulence that sent them crashing into each other. Colm bit back an oath and kissed her swiftly on the lips before putting her back in her seat and buckling the seatbelt tightly.

"I want you, girl," He gritted, tugging on the strap, making sure it was snug, "but I also want you safe. Tomorrow, we pick up where we left off, and that's a promise."

FOUR HOURS AND twenty minutes after they left Teterboro, the jet began its final descent.

It would not be a smooth landing, either, Ava thought, as the jet bounced and jumped, buffeted by the turbulence that kept most aircraft out of St. Barts' tiny airport. Apparently, the small island had an even smaller runway and private jets had to have a special license to land on St. Barts. Colm's pilot had been given the clearance when Colm bought the estate overlooking Lorient Bay.

All this, Ava knew, because Colm talked to her throughout the wild landing, talking to her to keep her from focusing on the crazy jolts and bumps.

She let him talk, too, welcoming the distraction. Not just from the rough air, but from him.

He was too attractive for his own good. The near kiss had woken something in her and she couldn't make the heat go away. She felt electric on the inside and painfully aware of Colm and how appealing she still found him. But how could she not? He was tall and muscular and beautifully shaped…the angle of his jaw, the distance between his shoulders, the length of his leg, the width of his hand.

She wanted to be back in his arms. She wanted to feel his hands. She wanted—

The jet het another pocket of rough air and did a dramatic shuddering bounce.

Her gaze went to Malcolm's. He smiled at her, reassuring, and she exhaled.

"Almost there," he said.

"You were right. It is bumpy."

"Almost always is."

She glanced from him, to the window. Yellow and red lights lined the island runway. She saw where the lights stopped. It was all darkness and then beyond white rolled against the dark. Waves, she thought. That must be the ocean beyond.

"Why did you buy the villa here?" she asked, glancing back at Colm, not wanting to think about what would happen if the jet overshot the runway.

"Seemed like a good investment at the time, but I didn't use it very often. There wasn't any point, and then a year ago Christmas, Jack and I came out and had a lot of fun, and we've been back several times. We spent Christmas here this year, too."

The jet touched down, the landing surprisingly smooth after the bumpy descent.

"We made it," she said, looking out the window as the jet taxied towards the small terminal building. Yellow lights lined the narrow tarmac. The moon shone high and full, outlining distant palm trees.

"Did you doubt it?" he asked, with a smile.

"I was just glad you looked calm. I would have been a wreck if you'd been nervous." She suddenly yawned and she lifted a hand to cover her mouth. "I am tired, though. What time is it?"

He glanced at his watch. "Almost midnight back home, so nearly one in the morning here.

No wonder she was sleepy. She was usually in bed by nine. Ava smothered another yawn. "Sorry. I don't know what's hit me."

"It's late. But don't worry. We'll have you in bed soon." He saw her sharp look and laughed. "Your bed. Relax. You're safe tonight."

Chapter Six

S HE WOKE UP with a start. The room was dark. Pitch black. Her room at home was never this dark. Where was she?

Ava leaned across the bed, reaching for a bedside lamp. She stretched as far as she could and touched the edge of a table before knocking a glass cylinder, nearly sending it crashing to the floor. She caught the glass pitcher and then bumped a smaller drinking glass, but no lamp.

Where was she?

What was happening?

She left the bed too quickly, and it was a longer way down and she landed heavily, awkwardly, and nearly cried out at the lash of pain shooting through her legs into her hip.

Her eyes burned and she swallowed hard.

Where, where, where….if she wasn't home, where was she?

She struggled to remember, to piece the last several days together. She'd remember the details if she calmed down.

She'd remember if she didn't panic. And yet it was hard not to panic when everything was blank, her mind was blank, all memory blank.

But it wasn't entirely blank. She knew she had an apartment, and she knew she was a dancer with the ballet company—

No. No. Not right. She was no longer a dancer. She'd been hurt. She couldn't dance anymore. But she worked for the ballet, teaching.

So, if she wasn't in New York…where was she?

She groped the wall, above the table, and finally she came upon a set of buttons. She pushed one, and then the other. The bedside lamp turned on. The overhead lights flooded the room with light.

She took it all in, trying to think, trying to remember.

It was all so strange.

Huge, cream wooden shutters lined one wall. The high coved ceiling was marked by an elegant ivory ceiling fan. Her bed was a giant four poster affair with shimmering rose and coral silk hangings. A pile of silk pillows in every shade of rose was stacked on the chest at the foot of her bed.

But none of it looked familiar. She didn't know why she was here. She didn't understand any of this.

Her bedroom door opened. Colm entered, wearing nothing but thin cotton pajama pants. "You okay, Ava?" he asked, his deep voice a sleepy rumble.

She shook her head. She knew him, of course she knew

him, she dreamed about him every night, dreamed of love won and lost, and lost, and lost…

"Where am I?" she whispered.

He was walking towards her, pushing back dark blonde hair from his forehead, muscles rippling in his chest, arm. "At my place. On St. Barts."

She looked from his hard, thickly muscled chest to the jutting angle of his jaw and then to his eyes. "How? Why?"

"You came with me last night."

It was her turn to push a tangle of hair from her face. Her hand was trembling. Her legs weren't at all steady. Her eyes burned, hot and dry, and painfully gritty. "I don't remember."

"We're here for a holiday."

"Why?"

"We thought it'd be fun to have a little R&R. You've always loved the sea, and it's warm here. Not at all like New York, which is in the middle of a snowstorm." He talked as he walked towards her, his pace slow, and body relaxed and yet she felt ripples of heat and tension.

Just watching him approach made her nervous, anxious. She backed up a step. And then another, bumping into the chest at the foot of the bed. "But why here, now?" She couldn't sort it out. "Why…now…?"

"You don't remember that I came to see you yesterday in New York? You were working at the school, teaching, and we talked about our son, Jack, and how much he misses you."

She winced at the mention of Jack. Jack, her baby. She didn't know him, though, not really. She'd only seen him a couple times because she wasn't a fit mother. She was dangerous. Colm had to keep her away.

"Is he okay?" she asked. "Has something happened?"

"No." Colm stopped just a few feet from her, hands resting low on his hips. He still looked relaxed, and yet she felt his scrutiny. He was studying her closely, monitoring her expression. "He's doing great. Healthy. Happy. You're the one we worry about."

Her heart ached. Air bottled in her lungs. "Why?"

"We miss you."

She continued to hold her breath, holding the pain and longing in. She'd been so lonely…she'd been so lost without them. "I miss him." She swallowed hard. *And you. I miss you so much,* she wanted to tell Colm, but couldn't. She was too broken, too damaged. She couldn't be what he wanted or needed and she had to be mature, had to accept how things were. She was better off alone. It was her only way to protect Jack, and Malcolm. Sometimes love meant sacrificing what you wanted in able to meet the needs of others.

"Only Jack?" He teased, firm mouth quirking, tone wry. "Not me? Not even a little bit?"

Always you.

I have loved you from the moment I first laid eyes on you.

She struggled to speak but a lump filled her throat and

she blinked to keep her eyes dry. "Maybe a little bit," she admitted hoarsely. *So much. Too much.*

"I'll take that," Colm said, moving another step towards her, closing the distance, bringing her against him. His hands settled on her shoulders before moving carefully down her back. He was warm, so warm. His touch soothed her, comforting her in a way words never could.

She tried to hold herself upright but his skin was a siren call and she needed him. Wanted him.

He stroked back up her back, drawing her even closer and finally she gave in, leaning against him, resting.

And once she was relaxed, her led her back to bed, and climbed into the bed with her, holding her until she fell asleep in his arms.

It took Colm far longer to fall back asleep.

AVA SIGHED WITH pleasure, warm and so very comfortable. Sleepily, she stretched, and as she stretched she encountered warm skin and hard muscle.

All sleepy thoughts vanished and she opened her eyes to discover it was morning, the wooden plantation shutters open, along with the oversized sliding glass doors, inviting the sunshine in. But that wasn't all. Colm was in the bed with her, lying on his back, arms folded behind his head. The covers were bunched low at his hips, exposing his broad, bare chest.

She didn't know where to look—his body or his face.

"What are you doing here?" she demanded, blushing, tugging the covers up higher, trying to cover him and her.

"You must have had a bad dream because you woke, and were upset, so I put you to bed, and stayed to be sure you were okay."

She pressed the covers to her collarbone. "You are so attentive," she said primly.

"I try."

"Hmph."

He smiled lazily. "You're really wrestling with those covers, Ava. It's almost as if you're a virgin." His smile reached his eyes. "In case you forgot, you're not."

She sat up, covers still pressed to her chest. "You can leave now."

"You're kicking me out of your bed now that I've served my purpose?"

She blushed all over again. "Nothing happened last night."

"How do you know?"

Her mouth opened, closed. That was a good question. Not that she'd tell him that. He was already looking a little too much like a big cat in her bed, and extremely self-satisfied. "I would know if something had happened."

"How so?"

"I would just know."

He rose up on his elbow to look at her. "So what about on the plane? What did we do during the flight?"

Ava slid out of bed, putting much needed distance between them. "Nothing." She saw his expression and hurriedly added. "We couldn't do anything. There was too much turbulence."

"So, you do remember the flight."

"You seem to be part of my emotional memory. For the good and the bad."

"I would prefer to think of it as good." He threw back the covers and stepped from bed. "Want coffee? Breakfast?"

"Coffee would be wonderful. Maybe a slice of toast, too."

"I'll have coffee and breakfast sent to you. They'll probably set your table on the deck out there. Is this alright with you?"

She nodded. "Are you not going to eat?"

"I'm going to go run and then I'll be back, and I'll have a light bite and then take you on a tour of the place."

WHEN COLM RETURNED an hour later, he found Ava on the deck, leaning against the railing, her long, dark hair loose, her slim figure wrapped in a delicate cherry silk robe that made her pale skin glow, and highlighted the hint of pink in her cheeks. He'd picked the robe up on one of his trips, thinking she'd looked gorgeous in it, and she did. But then, he thought she could wear a paper bag and be stunning.

She hadn't heard him yet and he watched her for a moment, feeling the same rush of possession and desire he always felt when near her.

He'd been smitten with her from the start. Only he hadn't always known how to tell her. Or maybe, he'd been too proud to tell her.

Had it been a game? A power trip?

God help him…he hoped not.

He made a sound, and she turned, spotted him, and gave him a smile. "How was the run?" she asked.

He joined at her the railing. "Good." He forced his gaze from her fine elegant features to the turquoise water and the foam tipped waves. It was a beautiful day and yet she was a hundred times more appealing. "Did you eat?"

"I did. More than I usually do."

"That's good."

"Dancers can't afford to gain weight, though."

"Not even dance teachers?"

"No." She grimaced. "I wouldn't be respected. That's why I write everything I eat down. Helps me keep track."

"Speaking of your notebook, Mickey found it in the car. He said he'd mail it, but with the weather, I'm thinking we will be home before it gets here."

"Then don't have him mail."

"We can go buy you a new one today if you'd like. I don't want you to worry while you're here."

"Maybe. Let's see how I do today. Maybe I'll be okay. Who knows? It'll be an adventure, right?"

"You're in a good mood."

"I am. I can't help it. It's gorgeous here." She lifted her

face to the sun, and sighed with pleasure. "And warm. I don't hurt. It's amazing."

"Feel up to a tour of the place?"

"This place is bigger than this one wing, isn't it?"

"You're in the main house now, and then there are four guest bungalows scattered around the property."

"How big is the property?"

"Five acres."

"Wow. That's huge."

"We're not going to see it all. I thought after you dress, we'd tour the main house, and then see the pool, so you know where to go to cool off."

EVERYTHING ABOUT THE main house was beautiful, the stone and crisp white wood a nod to the West Indies' architecture, with an open floor plan and walls of French doors that opened onto plantation-style verandas. Every room in the house had an ocean view, and a generous veranda. There were four bedrooms in the main house, two in each wing, and all four bedrooms had their own connecting bath. The master bedroom also had a mini bar with sink, refrigerator, and coffee pot tucked inside an alcove between the dressing room and bathroom.

The house was luxurious, without being cold or imposing. Ava loved it.

"And this is Jack's room," he said as they reached the third bedroom, but Ava stopped him before he opened the door.

"Maybe later," she said, her smile slipping, her buoyancy fading.

She couldn't bear to see the room—or life—of the son she couldn't be with. It'd hurt too much. Just knowing it was his bed, his clothes, his toys on the other side of the door made her want to run, scream, cry.

She'd failed her son. She'd failed all of them.

"I've tired you out," Colm said, sounding casual.

And yet he knew, she thought. He knew she was afraid. Or maybe he thought she really didn't care. Either way the guilt and shame engulfed her.

"I am tired," she said, and it was true. Her chest squeezed tight, making every breath a challenge. Her legs were weighted. She wasn't sure she could move another step. "I think I should go to my room and rest."

"Don't go to your room to hide. It's too early in the day."

"I'm not hiding. I just need to rest."

"Then come with me to the terrace. There are lounge chairs where you can put your feet up and relax without being alone in your room. The terrace has access to the pool as well as my favorite view of the bay."

"Maybe I need to be alone."

"Or maybe you're sad, or feeling the need to punish yourself."

Her head jerked up. She met his gaze. He gave her a

look.

"You do that," he added. "You're so hard on yourself. I don't know what you write in that little notebook of yours, but I imagine it's not always nice things. I have a feeling that along with your shopping lists or to-do lists are things like 'I'm a terrible person for losing Jack.'"

Her heart fell, and she went hot, then cold. "I *abandoned* him."

"I made mistakes that day, too. I left you two alone. I didn't warn the staff to supervise you. I allowed the situation to happen. But I refuse to spend the rest of my life hating myself, or blaming myself, for being human, just as I refuse to stand by and allow you to hate yourself, either. Things happen. So we deal with them."

She pressed her lips together, looked away, struggling with the different emotions rolling through her. His words didn't soothe. They just inflamed. "I don't want you to be my father. I don't want you to be this authority figure in my life."

"I'm speaking to you not as an authority figure but as your friend. Your lover—"

"Ha!"

"Your partner," he continued, ignoring her short mocking laugh. "We are two equals. Two halves of a whole. We have a responsibility to each other. To care for each other and be honest with each other as well."

"That sounds miserable."

He laughed low, the sound incredibly sexy. "It doesn't have to be. We can play. Have fun."

The husky note in his voice matched the heat in his eyes. Her pulse quickened. Her tummy flipped. "Not sure how to play anymore." Her voice was a little too breathless. Her legs felt a little too jelly-like.

"I remember how. I can show you."

His inflection made her flush. "I have a feeling that you're talking about sex."

"Sex is play. Sex is fun." He reached out and gently tugged on a long dark tendril of hair. "You are so beautiful. You deserve to play and have fun. You deserve to feel good…and gorgeous. When is the last time you felt good, Ava?"

Her heart was racing now. She pressed her knees together, trying to ignore the ache inside of her.

He found another tendril and then another, his hand sliding through her hair, playing with it. "Do you ever make yourself feel good? Do you ever—"

"*No.*" She gritted, flushing hotly and yet unable to look away from his gaze, transfixed by the intensity and fire in the glowing blue-green depths. It had been a long time since she felt good. It had been forever…

He reached for her, drawing her towards him. "Why not?"

"You're talking nonsense," she whispered, fighting to deny his effect on her, and failing. Her body was responding.

She was melting on in the inside, her skin sensitive, her breasts tender inside her bra, while deep between her legs she felt empty, hungry.

How could he do this so easily? Reduce her to a puddle of want?

HE WAS LEANING against the wall, his feet wide, and pulled her all the way between his feet, and, by drawing her forward, he took her weight, supporting her. "Let me make you feel good again, Ava," he murmured, tilting her head up and brushing his mouth across hers, once, and then again. "Your lips are so warm, so soft."

She closed her eyes at the fleeting kiss. Her heart galloped madly. "You are playing dirty."

"I've always gone after what I wanted. And I want you, Ava."

Once more his mouth covered hers, but this time the kiss was firm, insistent, and his lips parted hers, his tongue sweeping the soft fullness of her lower lip waking every nerve in her body. She shivered against him, feeling so much, remembering them, as they had been before she'd been hurt. It felt good—familiar—being in his arms and yet it was also overwhelming. Their relationship had always been so fiery. The physical had consumed both. They'd been passionate lovers, not friends, and maybe that was part of the problem in the months and years following the accident. They didn't know how to be anything but lovers, and that didn't work for them anymore.

"You mouth is so warm and sweet," he said. "It makes me think of how warm and soft you are between your thighs, and how much I love to kiss you there."

"You can't say that," she protested against his mouth.

"Oh, I can, just as I can still make you mine. I know you want me still." And then he set about proving his point, deepening the kiss, running the tip of his tongue along the seam of her lips, applying just the right amount of pressure, kissing her just the way she loved to be kissed, coaxing the response he wanted until she opened her mouth to him with a sigh.

His tongue swept inside her mouth, taking her, tasting her, sending darts of delicious sensation racing through her, as bright pricks of light exploded behind her eyelids, electrifying her from head to toe.

She'd forgotten this, the pleasure of a kiss.

She'd forgotten this, how good it felt to be touched, desired.

For the first time in ages, she felt wonderfully alive, tingling all over.

His head lifted briefly, his eyes were dark. "You can't deny this," he rasped, sweeping his thumbs across her cheekbones. "You can't deny us a chance."

She stared up at him, dazed, her senses stirred, her blood humming. It was virtually impossible to think, much less form a coherent thought. But she tried. She tried to remember why this was wrong, why this wouldn't work. "It's just…the physical."

He ran the pad of his thumb over her tender mouth, stroking ever so lightly in the middle of the soft, swollen lower lip, making her nerves tighten and dance. "Liar. You and I know carnal, babe, but this is more than sex. This is so intense because we're invested in each other. We want each other. We need each other." His thumb strummed her lip. "I need you, and you can say what you want, but I know you need me, too."

She opened her mouth to deny her attraction, deny him, but he wasn't having it. His head dipped, his mouth took hers, the kiss fierce, almost punishing. His tongue found hers and he drew her tongue into his mouth, sucking rhythmically on the tip, an exquisite tension that made her press against him, craving friction and relief, but he wasn't interested in soothing her. He wanted her to feel, and ache, and he was making sure she was hot. Wet.

And she was hot, so hot, a thick honey in her veins, her panties growing damper against her skin. If he touched her, she'd be slick, and ready for him. She was always ready for him. It was impossible to resist him. She'd always been putty in his hands. But it wasn't a good thing. He was her weakness. Still.

If she had any sense, she'd pull away now. She'd utter a sharp rebuke, and reject him soundly.

But she wanted this. She wanted everything she'd missed,

and when his hand went to her jaw, angling her head to give him even deeper access to her mouth, she trembled with need.

His palm slid down her throat, fingers finding nerves she didn't even know she had. Ava leaned against him, dazzled by the riot of sensation and the sharp, insistent desire. It had been over a year since they'd last made love, but the hunger was still there, a feverish wanting that charged every kiss, every touch.

No one had ever made her feel so much.

No one had ever made her want so much.

Sensation rippled through her, followed by waves of bittersweet pleasure. He was claiming her with the kiss, reminding her she'd always been his, and would always be his, and she couldn't deny it, not when he melted her from the inside out and her body ached for his hands and touch, needing his body and the release.

His head lifted and he gazed down into her face, his features hard, his expression fiercely possessive. "You still want me," he rasped.

"That's never been the issue," she answered, breathing fast, dazed by the explosive chemistry.

"Then that's a start," he retorted, gently pulling her away and then stepping back a foot. "I can work with that."

Ava swayed on her feet, dazed, lips and body pulsing.

From the heat of the kiss, she'd expected Colm to either take her here, in the hall, or carry her off into the nearest bedroom and ravish her, but instead he was backing off. Right when she was ready for more.

She smoothed her sundress and struggled to gain control over her breathing, but it was still ragged. She felt ragged.

As well as hot. And hungry.

He'd made her want more, and yet now he was pulling away.

So not fair.

Frustrated, she looked up at him and their gazes locked. She realized from his expression he knew exactly how she felt. He'd done this deliberately. Turned her on. And then backed off.

"That was dirty," she said hoarsely.

"Not dirty. We're playing."

"In that case, we have a very different definition of playing."

He laughed softly. "I don't think so. I just think you're out of practice. Pleasure isn't something to be rushed. Desire needs to be stirred—"

"Oh, it's stirred."

"And senses need to be teased."

"You've done that as well."

His lips twitched. "So enjoy the anticipation. That's half of the pleasure."

"Mmm. Great. I can't wait."

His eyes glinted with amusement. "Go change into one of the swimsuits in your closet, and then meet me at the pool. We can cool off with a swim before lunch is served on the terrace."

"You're awfully bossy, Colm."

"Just wait until I get you into bed."

Chapter Seven

THEY SWAM AND splashed about the pool for a half hour and then lay on the plush lounge chairs, soaking up the sun for another half hour. They were still relaxing when staff appeared and set the table on the veranda.

It was a joy to eat lunch outside with the stunning view of the rocky, green hills that gave way to the dazzling turquoise water. It was warm without being too hot. And the seafood lunch was perfectly flavored. Ava ate more than she usually did and could tell Colm approved.

"I'm glad you're eating" he said, as she finished the prawn salad. "I hate that you have spent most of your life starving yourself to stay ballerina thin. Your life has been about constant deprivation."

"I try not to think of it that way. It's not deprivation. It's a discipline."

"Do you still count every little calorie?"

"If I had my notebook here, yes."

"Why?"

"It's habit."

"But you're so slender, Ava. You could stand to gain five, ten, fifteen pounds, and your body needs protein, vitamins, nutrients. You need to eat real food, good for your body and soul, food."

She grimaced. "You're a bit of a nag, you know."

"I refuse to be offended."

She shook her head, smiling. "That's fine, but, just know, I can't spend all four days here eating and drinking. There must be moderation."

"We did swim, and walk a little."

"It is gorgeous here." She glanced around, taking in the lush landscaping of palms, white hibiscus, and bougainvillea in shades of white, pink, and purple. "The view is incredible, but it's also surprisingly peaceful." Growing up, her family had a beach house in Mar del Palata on Argentina's Atlantic coast, but that was truly a house on the beach while Colm's villa was part of a sprawling estate on a side of a mountain. The beach wasn't anywhere nearby. In fact, she wasn't sure he even had beach access. "If you want to go to the beach, where do you go?"

"We have our own beach down below."

"How do you get there?"

"There's a little gondola that whisks guests up and down the mountain."

"You're joking!"

"No. It was here when I bought the estate, and I'm glad,

because what is the point of having a Caribbean getaway if you don't have a private beach?"

"A five-acre estate, with four guest bungalows and a private gondola must have been a serious chunk of change. Dare I even ask how much it was?"

"You'd be disgusted. A ridiculous extravagance, but it did help a friend."

"Fifteen million."

"Far more disgusted than that."

Her eyes widened. "Over twenty?"

"You're still off by quite a bit."

"Colm!"

"I thought you'd like the gondola."

"Don't even put that on me. That's absurd."

"It's an investment, and it'll hold its value. St. Barts is the hot spot in the Caribbean, and has been for years—" He broke off as a young woman in a tailored, dove gray dress approached. "I have a surprise for you," he said to Eva. "This is Genevieve, and she's your assistant for the next few days."

Ava shot Colm a quick, worried glance. "Why do I need an assistant?"

"To make sure you're comfortable," he answered.

"But I am already," Ava protested.

"She'll make you even more comfortable."

"Is that possible?"

"Genevieve used to work for a very exclusive spa in Switzerland. She's an expert in pampering and she has something

planned for you this afternoon while I sit in on some confer-
ence calls with New York. Don't be nervous. This is
supposed to be fun, so go with her now, and I'll see you later
this afternoon, for cocktails and dinner."

Colm had meant to be reassuring but Ava's stomach
knotted as she followed Genevieve down a garden path
towards one of the guest bungalows.

"You're here to relax," Genevieve said cheerfully, leading
the way up the steps and into a spacious room decorated in
tropical pinks, greens, and coral with a breathtaking view of
the turquoise sea. "Mr. McKenzie has insisted everything be
perfectly pleasurable, and that's exactly how it shall be."

Ava watched Genevieve open a door to an adjacent bath.

"There's a robe here for you," Genevieve added, walking
briskly through the pink and white marble bath that looked
almost like a sweet confection, and gestured to a plush, pale
pink robe hanging on a gold hook next to the enormous glass
shower. "Why don't you shower and then slip into the robe.
Don't put anything on under your robe. Once dressed, come
out and I'll take you to the garden?"

"The garden?" Ava repeated, feeling foolish, and terribly
out of her element. She'd be better off in New York right
now. She wasn't good at this sort of thing. She didn't know
how to relax anymore. Nor could she afford to relax. Bad
things happened if she let down her guard. She missed her
notebook and her lists and her focus more than ever right
now.

But Genevieve was oblivious to Ava's discomfort and set about opening the rest of the sliding plantation shutters to allow more afternoon sunshine to flood the high ceilinged bathroom, revealing a private walled garden off the bath. The walled garden teemed with tropical flowers and a linen covered massage table stood in the midst of the lush greenery. "We'll do the massage outside. It's perfectly private so you can relax, and then after the massage, we have a pedicure and manicure planned, and then your hair."

There really must be something wrong with her, Ava thought, looking longingly towards the hall and the front door, when all she wanted to do was run away rather than give herself over to a proper massage. "This isn't necessary. I'm really not used to much fuss."

"Exactly. Which is why Mr. McKenzie wants you to be fussed over. He insists you be pampered and spoiled and treated like royalty, and that is just what I intend to do."

"I've got scars."

"My early training was at a rehabilitation hospital in Zurich. Many of those I worked with were paralyzed. I have seen it all, trust me."

Ava wasn't very good at trusting anyone anymore, but once on the massage table Ava had to admit that Genevieve was very good at what she did. Ava had forgotten the bliss of a good massage. There was power in touch, power in being treated gently, kindly, and Ava's tension and anxiety melted as Genevieve kneaded, massaged, and applied fragrant oils, followed by cool soothing towels and lotions.

Several hours later, still bundled in the plush robe but with her skin glowing, hair shampooed and blow-dried, and nails freshly polished, Ava faced a huge walk-in closet filled with clothes she'd never seen before.

"Mr. McKenzie had them made for you," Genevieve explained, flicking on the closet light. "They're all top designers, and rather fun clothes, don't you think?"

Fun? How about impractical? Silk pants, skimpy beaded tops, short skirts, long slim skirts, sheer chiffon blouses that showed far too much of everything.

"I think they're a bit short on fabric," Ava said, holding up a rich amethyst silk camisole that was also nearly backless and a narrow long skirt with a thigh-high slit.

"You've an amazing figure. Might as well show it off. Besides, there's no one here to see but Mr. McKenzie."

Ava's stomach did a wild dive. Precisely her worry. She wasn't the same woman she'd been before the accident. She didn't have her old grace, lacked the fluid gestures and easy elegance that had come from years of dance training in Buenos Aires. She might not need the walker or cane, but she was far from sexy.

Ava returned the purple silk outfit to the hanger. "I think something more conservative. Black. High neck."

Genevieve shook her head. "You won't find anything like that here. Mr. McKenzie made sure of that. But this shade of purple will look fantastic on you. Let's get you dressed."

It was almost dusk when Genevieve led Ava back down the long, garden path, from one flagstone path to another. The garden was lit with dozens of colorful, Chinese lanterns, making the garden look like a little jewel box.

They reached a stone patio and in the center was a dark red gondola. Another member of Malcolm's staff stood at attention. "Your carriage," Geneieve said with a smile. "Mr. McKenzie is waiting for you down below."

THE GONDOLA RIDE took several minutes. It was definitely not a fast trip down the hillside, but with the sun beginning to set, it was beautiful. As they neared the beach, she spotted a white cabana and dozens of candles and tiki torches providing flickering light.

Colm was indeed waiting for her at the bottom. She could see him as the gondola approached, his shadow stretching long on the sand, silhouetted by the setting of the red-gold sun.

Her stomach did a wild somersault and she pressed a hand to her belly, her nerves getting the better of her.

He opened the door to the gondola when it came to a stop and then lifted her onto the still warm sand. "You look amazing," he said, leaving his hands on her waist.

She could feel the heat of his skin against hers through her thin, silk camisole. It was exciting and yet overwhelming. Being with Colm was overwhelming. Everything here in St. Barts was so new, and there were so many experiences and she couldn't catalogue them and remember the details and she knew she wouldn't remember everything tomorrow.

She'd remember Colm, of course. But she might not remember this...the gondola ride, the sunset, the seductive warmth of his hands against her waist.

"Don't worry so much," he said, kissing her forehead.

"I'm scared."

"Why?"

"This is all so magical and you've gone to so much work to make it special but I might not remember any of it tomorrow. I won't remember how hard you've worked to make me comfortable, to help me relax."

"You don't have to remember that."

"But I do."

"No. You don't. You just have to enjoy yourself tonight. Live now. Be happy now. We'll worry about tomorrow, tomorrow."

Tears started to Ava's eyes. She felt so much just then, so many intense emotions. She desperately wanted to be the woman Colm deserved. He was a good man, and so very good to her. Loyal, passionate, fiercely protective. "I just want to remember the happy things...the good things. You know how my memory is...you know how fleeting the present is."

"Then we will become clever at capturing the good things. We will find ways to help you remember your life and all that which is hopeful and happy."

"How?"

"We will look for sunsets every night. We will celebrate life and our blessings. We will take photos and write down the funny things and the happy moments and we will make sure to live, really live. We can do that."

"The camera is probably a good idea. But I'm sorry you have to work so hard for me. I hate that you have to be clever just to help me remember. So much effort...so much trouble."

"It's not trouble. I've been looking forward to this all afternoon and the wait was worth it. You look amazing." And then he smiled, a very slow, sexy smile that made her knees knock and belly flip and for a split-second she felt absolutely gorgeous. "How do you feel? Good?"

"Very good. Genevieve was pretty sensational. I don't think I've ever had a better massage."

"I could give you a better one—"

"No. You'd get distracted by the girl bits and end up massaging the wrong parts."

He laughed. "You would have enjoyed it, though."

"Yes, but I don't know how relaxing it would have been."

"Well, you have would been relaxed after."

"Hmm." But she was smiling as she blushed. "We seem to discuss sex a lot."

"That's because we enjoyed sex a lot." He shot her a swift glance as he took her arm to lead her across the sand to the cabana. "Or do you not remember?"

"No, I do remember that. Maybe that's what makes me nervous. It seems as if we were just interested in the physical aspect of a relationship." She was grateful for his arm as the thick, soft sand gave way beneath each foot, making it difficult to keep her balance. "Am I wrong?"

"Not wrong." He walked her to a low couch, and made sure she was sitting comfortably before turning to open the champagne chilling on ice. "Does that bother you? That we were so physical?"

Ava blushed, her skin growing hot all over. She shifted one of the soft silk pillows, giving herself more room. "I just worry that it might not be enough. Or that it isn't enough…and I don't remember."

He didn't immediately reply, focusing instead on easing the cork from the green bottle. The cork popped and he filled one flute, and then the other.

"We were good together," he said simply, handing her a flute. "We enjoyed each other. I'm not sure either of us analyzed it." He faced her, big, imposing. So very self-assured.

Truly they were a study in opposites, she thought. He had everything and she…well, it was probably better to leave that alone.

"At least, I never did," he added. "It was enough that I liked you, and wanted you, and wanted to be with you whenever our schedules permitted."

She listened to what he was saying, and yet something rang false and she couldn't figure out what wasn't right. What wasn't true.

He was here before her—tall, handsome, successful. Ridiculously successful. If he bought an island estate for twenty-four million dollars, he could probably buy and sell small kingdoms if he wanted.

And he said he wanted her. *Her.*

It didn't make sense. And no, her memory wasn't what it used to be, but she still had logic, and logic made her question a relationship where she had never once heard him mention the word love.

If he didn't love her, then why was he so loyal?

If he didn't love her, why hadn't he moved on?

Was it because of Jack? Was it Jack he loved so much?

"What are you thinking?" he asked, brow creasing.

"Am I so transparent?"

"You don't hide your emotions like you used to."

"I'm not sure what that means."

He sat down next to her on the couch. "You used to keep your emotions under lock and key. You didn't like to show any weakness."

"And yes, emotions were a weakness."

"*If* you thought they'd be used against you." He hesitated. "You were that way from the time I met you. That wasn't a you and me thing, but an Ava thing. I always wondered if that came from dance, or maybe before that. If it was something you learned at home, as a girl in Argentina."

She looked down into her glass and watched the bubbles rise and fizz. "I think that is a Galvan thing," she murmured. "My father was not as easy man. The only way to survive was to protect yourself."

"I can relate."

Ava curled her legs under her. "I think our fathers were similar. Didn't they both divorce our mothers and marry younger women and have more children?"

He touched the edge of his goblet to hers. "Here's to remembering the good stuff."

She laughed at his sardonic humor. "I think you used to make me laugh, too."

"A lot. Even though I've been told I don't have a good sense of humor. Fortunately, you liked mine."

"I think it's because I liked you," she said softly, feeling the past, and the intensity of her love.

She'd adored him. She'd been crazy about him. He was the one with reservations. He was the one who hadn't wanted her…

Ava frowned and took a quick drink from her glass. The champagne was cold and crisp and it warmed as it went down.

He hadn't wanted her.

He hadn't wanted the baby, either.

That was the reason they'd had that fight. That was the fight on that last night, the one when she'd been hurt.

Or did she have it wrong?

It wasn't something she'd put in her notebook. It wasn't something she could read there. It wasn't something anyone had told her, either. But it whispered through her, and the whisper had shape and weight. Truth.

"I can see the wheels turning," he said, reaching out to lift one of her long strands of hair, and curling the ends around his finger. "What are you worrying about now?"

"Facts." She struggled to smile but couldn't. A lump was forming in her throat making it hard to swallow. "Details. Things like that."

"Those must be very distressing facts because you look very sad now. Can you share those facts and details with me?"

But she couldn't. She was afraid to hear what he had to say. Afraid that everything about this evening would change. And it was—or it had been—magical. The gondola ride. The tent on the beach. The candles and flickering torches.

"It's nothing." She sipped her champagne, swallowing a mouthful because she needed the fizz and burn. He didn't love her. He'd never loved her.

He was raising Jack out of guilt.

And that was why he wanted her back. Not because he wanted her, but because he was driven by guilt.

It felt like a fireball exploded in her chest. Her heart burned. Her throat ached. Pain rushed through her.

She turned her head and looked at him, unable to keep

the words to herself. "You never loved me." She said the words brokenly, bluntly. "You didn't want Jack, either. I did."

His hand fell from her hair. He leaned back against the couch cushion, his jaw tightening, hardening. "It's not that black and white. It never was."

"We fought the night of the accident. We fought about the baby."

"Yes." Colm's voice was clipped.

She studied his hard features. His expression was shuttered. There was no more light or easy warmth in his eyes.

"If it's not black and white, then tell me what happened." She couldn't look away from his face, wanting to understand, needing to make sense of a past that constantly slipped away.

"Will it matter tomorrow?" he retorted, looking at her. "Will you remember? You don't have your notebook to write down the truth."

She flinched. "That was a low blow."

"It's not—" He broke off, and in one smooth motion, rose to his feet.

He stalked to the edge of the flat Turkish carpet that had been rolled across the sand and for a long minute he stood, facing the sea, his shoulders rigid, posture stiff.

She could feel his anger and frustration. This was the Colm she knew. The warrior. The raider. The one victor who took no prisoners.

The silence added to the tension until her insides churned.

Finally he turned around to face her. "You never remember the good, Ava. You never remember what I did right. You only remember what I did wrong. And you're right. We did fight that night, and I put you into the cab after our fight and I let you leave in tears. I watched you go after we exchanged harsh words and our world has never been the same. We have never been the same. And I blame myself, every single day. Every day. Especially when I'm with our boy and he looks up at me with dark brown eyes that are your eyes, and he asks me about you with this grave expression that is so you, and he wonders where you are. Where his mama is. And it slays me, every single day, Ava. Every day, I ask God to forgive me for being caught off guard that night, for not celebrating your pregnancy the way I should have celebrated the life we made. I am sorry. And I've told you I am sorry so many times but you never remember."

He dragged a hand across his face, rubbing across his eyes and then down to his jaw. "And I've tried, I've tried to make it right and I can't. And I don't know how else to make it better but I do love him. And I love you—"

"Now," she whispered faintly. "You love me now."

"Yes."

"But you didn't love me then."

His jaw worked, tightening, then easing. "I must have because I have fought for you every day since."

"But that night…the night of the accident…you didn't love me. Did you?"

"Does it matter?"

She set the champagne down. "I loved you."

He stared at her and she could tell he didn't know what to say. Which was maybe a good thing. She didn't know what to say, either.

"This is why we're not together," she murmured, speaking more to herself then him. "This is the reason. Not Jack. I love Jack." She looked up at him, her gaze searching his. "I have always loved Jack. I have always wanted to protect him. But you…you wanted me to get rid of him. You wanted me to end the pregnancy."

"That night, that fight, is three and a half years ago. I have been a father every night since then, at your side when you were in a coma, there the night they delivered Jack. I cut his umbilical cord. I walked with him every night when he was a five pound newborn. I fed him every two hours for three months until he could manage to sleep in four hour stretches. I do regret my words, but its time you focused on my actions. I do love Jack, and I do love you. But you don't remember any of that, either."

She struggled to her feet. "You speak with so much scorn."

"You're not the only one who is tired, Ava. I'm tired, too. This is hard. Making this work, it's not always easy. I've waited months to try again with you, but it's tough when you fling a past that is three and a half years old in my face."

Her thoughts raced so fast it was impossible to pick the

right words. Instead, she clenched and unclenched her hands. If she could run, she'd run. She'd run far away from here. But her body didn't run anymore and her mind wasn't what it used to be. She didn't know how to be clever or evasive. She was just who she was.

Damaged. Broken. Flawed.

"I shouldn't have come," she said, heart thudding so hard she felt like throwing up.

"Don't say that."

"But it's true. And I'm sorry. I'm sorry I don't remember, and I'm sorry I'm stuck in the past. I wish I had more memories, newer memories, but there's that break…the before, and after. I remember mostly the before."

"Please don't apologize."

"I have to. I'm ashamed—"

"Christ, Ava, please, please don't say that." He went to her, swiftly closing the distance and he pulled her against him. "Say anything but that."

She closed her eyes as his arms went around her. He felt familiar but unfamiliar and this time she knew why.

She loved him.

She hated him.

She needed him.

She couldn't bear to be with him.

He made her hurt. He made her ache. He made her wish she'd never met him…

Chapter Eight

COLM WENT TO the table and picked up her flute and handed it back to her. "Come, sit down. There's no point in fighting. It's not going to accomplish anything."

Her chin jerked up and she stared at him defiantly. "Don't be condescending."

"I'm not. I'm trying to salvage the evening. It was supposed to be a nice evening. I was hoping to create some good memories for you."

She drew a quick breath and then exhaled slowly. "With any luck, I won't remember tonight." And then she made a face. "That was a joke."

He smiled crookedly. "I know. And it was a good one."

"But knowing my luck, I won't forget."

"Another joke."

"Pretty good, huh? Next thing you know and I'll be out on the comedy circuit."

He laughed softly, appreciating the levity, appreciating her. She was such a little thing—the top of her head didn't even reach his shoulder—but she was fierce. Fiesty. His Argentine beauty.

"Can we start tonight over? Try this again?" he asked.

"Maybe." She extended a hand to him. "I'm Ava."

"I'm Colm."

"It's nice to meet you, Colm. Do I detect an accent?"

"I was raised in Scotland."

"I was raised in Argentina."

"What brought you to the US, Ava?"

"Ballet. I'm a dancer—" She broke off, corrected. "Was a dancer. I just teach now. What about you?"

"I buy things, sell things, make money."

"Is that your passion? Money?"

"No. I'm just really good at it. Is dance your passion?"

"Yes. I love it. I do." She looked up at him, her gaze examining his face. "I also have a passion for brawny blondes with a Scottish accent. You can blame it on Diana Gabaldon. The Highlander."

His lips quirked. "I believe the story is *The Outlander.*"

"Ah, right. Well. This might be a good time to mention that I was in a car accident in New York and hit my head pretty good. So there's some brain trauma, and memory issues, and balance problems, and pain, but other than that, I'm really good." She smiled up at him. "Any questions?"

"None at all."

"Good. Because it looks like you have an army of staff arriving with dinner."

AFTER THE EARLIER drama, dinner was relatively uneventful.

There was no more fighting. The tension was gone. They'd come to an understanding of sorts.

Ava wasn't sure what the understanding was. Maybe they were just too mellow from the champagne, or maybe the fact that they were eating by candlelight in an elegant tent on the beach made them feel civilized.

Or, perhaps, the torches ringing the tent's perimeter had them feeling like castaways on a tropical island…

Or, maybe, just maybe, they were enjoying each other's company.

Imagine that.

Ava sipped her coffee and lounged against the soft silk pillows lining the couch, watching the flame dance on a torch just outside the cabana. The flame was matched by the flickering candles on the table. It had been a gorgeous meal. She couldn't remember when she'd last eaten so well, or been served on such fine china or toasted with such excellent crystal.

"Did we take a picture of this?" she asked, turning to look at Colm. "If not, we should. I want to remember this. It's like you're Valentino and we're in our very own desert oasis. Except, we're not in the desert but on a private beach with a view of the sea."

He grinned. His teeth flashed whitely. "You're funny."

"You bring it out in me."

Colm leaned forward, checked her wine glass. His eyes

were brilliant in the candlelight. "You're empty. Want more?"

"No, I'm happy with my coffee. I have enough trouble without a hangover." She smiled at him. "Thank you. For this. It really was lovely."

"It turned out okay."

"Despite the bumpy start."

"We've always had bumps, babe. We're strong people. We knock heads. Have different opinions. But it's what makes us, us."

She held his gaze a moment and then set her cup down. "Can I ask you something?"

"Sure."

"Have we ever been friends?"

Colm opened his mouth then closed it. He gave his head a brief shake. "I don't know how to answer that."

"Which makes me think the answer is no."

His brow furrowed. "Relationships are complicated."

"Or are we complicated?"

He made a soft, rough sound. "I've always said you are the smartest woman I've ever met."

She gave him a look. "And still you avoid the question. Never a good sign."

"I want to be honest with you, and I'm trying." He leaned forward, wrapped his hand around her neck and drew her towards him, kissing her hard, and then soft, and then slow, hot, and demanding as the kiss sparked and desire exploded and the kiss went on and on until she was boneless and mindless and a tingling mass of nerves.

"We were not then what we are now," he said, stroking her full soft lip with the pad of his thumb. "We didn't talk about much. You had dance. I had my work. We met late at night, and, if lucky, we slept together until early in the morning when you left for the theater. But there were plenty of days—weeks—where I traveled or the Manhattan Ballet traveled and we would text or call, but those calls would be brief. There wasn't much to say. We didn't share feelings. We didn't talk too much about work. We communicated in bed. We expressed ourselves through sex."

She caught his thumb, stopped its maddening caress so she could try to complete a thought. "And you never wanted more from me?"

He hesitated only briefly. "No."

"Did you ever want more from any woman?"

"What is this about, Ava? I'm not sure I understand."

She searched his eyes, trying to see past the startling color to the man behind. Their relationship baffled her. She wondered if it had always baffled her. She imagined so, but couldn't be sure. Maybe before the accident she'd been happy with what he gave her...maybe the sex had been enough.

Or maybe it hadn't. Maybe the unexpected pregnancy had jolted them out of complacency....

"I search my memory and you are there," she said, holding his hand, "but there is very little attached to you. You are just there. Big, handsome, sexual...but I can't find a relationship. I don't have stories. I don't have lots of pictures. If anything, I just see you and me, in bed."

"That is where we were happiest." He hesitated. "And you were happy with me, Ava. You were happy with us. At least, you were happy until our fight that night. That night wasn't good. You said things. I said things. You stormed out. I happily put you into the cab. And then the taxi crashed and you were hurt and we have both lived with that night, hanging over us, haunting us, ever since."

"And the fight was about the baby."

"The pregnancy."

She mulled his choice of words over. She thought about the relationship and what she'd felt for him, and how she'd imagined he felt for her. She must have discovered the night they'd fought that he didn't have strong feelings for her. That he didn't want her, or the baby. Or maybe he'd given her an ultimatum. She didn't know. She might never know. Could she live with that?

ON HER SECOND night on the island, she slept better than she had in years, cocooned by soft French linens, clouds of down, and the gentle breeze of the ceiling fan. Ava didn't wake until Genevieve opened the plantation shutters and let in the golden sun.

"Good morning, Ms. Galván. It's going to be another

beautiful day. Mr. McKenzie hopes you'll join him in half an hour for breakfast on the yacht."

"The yacht?"

Genevieve smiled. "I've packed your swimsuit and a cover up in a tote since it sounds like you'll be doing some swimming later, too."

AVA DRESSED FOR the day on the yacht in a slim, white knit skirt and a white tank. She let Genevieve do her hair and was pleased by the loose but stylish ponytail.

Once she was ready to go, Genevieve drove Ava to the gondola platform in one of the estate's small golf carts to keep Ava from having to walk too much too early in the day.

Colm was waiting for her at the bottom of the gondola and he escorted her across the beach to a small motorboat waiting to ferry them out to the yacht anchored in the bay.

Ava was delighted to be out on the water and laughed as the motorboat hit a wave and gave them a light splash. In Argentina, she'd spent a lot of time on the water as a girl, and being here was bringing back memories of her family, and the holidays at the sea.

"Happy?" Colm asked as the boat neared the anchored yacht.

She nodded. "I love this. Reminds me of home."

On the yacht, Colm took her on a brief tour so she'd have her bearings and then they took seats at a table on one of the back decks to take advantage of the morning sun.

It was a perfect morning, warm but not hot with just a few puffy white clouds to highlight the azure sky.

Staff appeared with pitchers of fresh squeezed juices and pots of strong black coffee and then followed with platters of eggs and grilled tomatoes and breakfast meats. Ava focused on coffee and a delicate croissant, while Colm ate a little bit of everything.

They didn't talk much over breakfast, content to just enjoy the meal, the sun, and the passing scenery. It was a spectacular way to see the island. From the water, St. Barts was a jagged sweep of green circled by white sand and lapping blue waves.

"This isn't real," she said. "I don't feel real. I'm not even sure you're real."

"Let me check that," he said, and before she knew what was happening, he'd dipped his head and kissed her.

A shiver of pleasure raced through her at the touch of his lips. He tasted good, warm, and she shivered again as the tingle of sensation gave way to heat. She always forgot how quickly the fire between them ignited, and it ignited now, hotter than ever.

By the time Colm lifted his head, her heart was racing and she felt positively electric.

How could one small kiss be hot and cold? How could it burn? How could it make her feel so painfully alive?

"It seems real enough to me," he answered lazily.

She flushed, battling emotion. She wanted more even as

she knew more wasn't good for her…or them.

"You look great today," he added. "But then, I've always liked you in white. It sets off your gorgeous hair and eyes."

"Thank you."

"You've begun to exercise again, haven't you?"

She glanced down, taking in the short skirt and length of bare leg. From this angle she couldn't see the scars but even if she could, she was determined not to let them upset her. "I'm dancing," she said. "Nothing complicated. Just beginner classes a couple days a week, but it feels good to be at the barre. Who knew I loved plies and tendus so much?"

"I did. And I'm glad you're taking classes again. It's good for you. Not just for your body. But your head." He leaned back as the staff cleared the last of the breakfast dishes. "Speaking of your head, you seemed to have slept well last night."

She frowned, puzzled. "Do you know something I don't?" she asked uneasily.

"I was with you last night."

"I didn't realize." She stiffened and then swallowed hard, suddenly wanting to be anywhere but here. How could she not have known? "Did I…did we…?"

"We didn't make love. We didn't even kiss. You were worried about waking up and not knowing where you were, so I stayed with you. That's all."

But she wasn't reassured. It was troubling for her, deeply troubling—even terrifying—to not know things, much less remember significant details like sharing a bed with some-one.

Or remembering where one left one's son.

Her eyes burned. She blinked back tears before they could fall. "This is why I did not want to come here. This is why I begged you to leave me in New York, to leave me with my routine. I hate forgetting things. I hate waking up and being lost and confused. But most of all, I hate that I can't remember what is important. You. Jack. And yet I do. And I always will."

"Maybe, but maybe not. You are better, Ava. Much, much better. And you know it." He leaned towards her, his big body invading her space, making the hair on her nape rise and her skin prickle with awareness. "Look at you. You're beautiful. And you're happy here. And, Ava, you'd be even happier with Jack."

He pushed an envelope towards her. He'd kept it hidden under the placemat but wanted her to have it now. "You don't have your notebook here, but if you did, I'd have you put these in it. To remember how you are. Not how you imagine yourself to be."

Her hands trembled as she opened the envelope and withdrew a half dozen photos. There were snapshots taken of the beach and sunset, another one of the tent, glowing with fresh flowers and candlelight, and then there were four of her, talking, laughing, smiling, and then just of one looking off towards the horizon, her expression thoughtful, perhaps a little wistful, but there was no pain in her features, no tension in her expression.

"You are this woman, Ava. Beautiful. Intelligent. Passionate. Proud. Funny. Regal. I could go on." He tipped her chin, looked into her eyes. "And you are ours…you are important and necessary to our family. We need you."

A lump filled her throat and she pulled away and glanced down at the photos she'd spread in a half circle on the table.

One wouldn't know she'd been so badly hurt from looking at these photos. She could see what Colm saw. The thick, long hair, tumbling down her back. The wide expressive eyes. The curve of her generous mouth. The slim shoulder and the skin pale and creamy against the rich plum of the silk camisole.

On the outside was beautiful, but the external beauty hid her damaged mind. And it was damaged. Every day she woke up and had to discover herself again. Every day she had to come to terms with whom she was, and what she now was, and if it exhausted her, how could it not exhaust Colm? And how could it not eventually embarrass her son?

She didn't want to cause Jack more pain. Hadn't she hurt him enough already?

She tapped the shot of her curled up on the couch, staring out at the horizon.

"I don't remember you taking these," she said softly.

"It was near the end of the evening. You took a couple of me. And then we took one together. A selfie."

"A selfie? How indulgent of us," she teased if only to hide the pain. She would go through life and not remember it. She'd go through life and forget everything that made life life.

"We had fun last night."

She struggled to smile, not wanting him to see the tears that were making her eyes sting and grow gritty. "I'll have to trust you on that."

"That's why I took the pictures. I wanted you to have memories—"

"But I don't remember. They are your memories, not mine."

He looked at her for a long moment, and he seemed to be choosing his words with care. "You don't remember anything of last night?"

She chewed on her bottom lip, working the tender skin over. "I had a massage and Genevieve did my hair and helped me dress."

"Yes."

"And I took the gondola down, to the beach."

"Yes."

"We ate there." She nodded to the photo of the tent. She frowned as she stared at the pictures. "I don't remember what we ate. I don't remember what we talked about, either."

"But you remember meeting me on the beach, and having dinner with me."

She nodded. "Yes."

"Do you remember how you felt?"

She hesitated a long moment. "I think I was happy. Maybe. I think I was also unhappy." She nudged a photo, sliding it over another. "Did we fight?" she asked, looking up at him.

"No. Why?"

"Because I think…I feel…there was something…something that wasn't happy."

"We talked about the accident last night. We talked about us, and how we were before the accident, and the fight we had the night of the accident." •

He'd spoken calmly, casually but each word felt like a blow. She put a hand to her chest, rubbing at the knot of pain. "That's why I was unhappy. We were fighting because you didn't want Jack, and I did, and yet because I got hurt, you have Jack and I don't, and we both feel guilty."

"You're remembering something that was years ago. That's not who we are today. We've changed. We're a family—"

"No."

"We are, and instead of you relying on your notebook for everything, I'm going to start taking pictures and showing you pictures and showing you what you don't see…that you're loved and wanted, but even more so, you're needed. I need you. Jack needs you—"

"Stop."

"You might not remember everything, but you are still you. Interesting, complex, beautiful. A miracle. Even the doctors agree that you are a marvel of modern medicine. Which is why you're here. I'm not going to allow you to give up."

"I haven't given up! Look at me—I'm working, teaching, living. But at the same time, I know my limitations. I have a routine, and I've created order and structure, and I stick with that order and structure. I don't try to multitask anymore. I'm realistic. You need to be realistic, too."

"You didn't become a principal with the ballet by being realistic."

"That was the past. We know I'm not that Ava anymore."

"Life isn't about sulking in shadows, playing it safe. We have to take risks. And in this case, it's a risk absolutely worth taking." His voice dropped, deepening, feathering up and down her spine the way his hands used to travel the length of her. "Jack's worth it, Ava. You know he is."

She gasped for a breath, heart tumbling.

Jack.

Jack was the best part of her. Gorgeous, gorgeous little boy, her miracle boy, the miracle she thanked God for every day. But at the same time, she had to protect him. She had to protect him from *her.* He could have died that day she abandoned him in his stroller. He could have been kidnapped, or murdered—

"Yes, bad things could have happened that day," Colm interrupted, able to read her emotions. "But they didn't. Security found him. I was able to get him. Everything turned out fine."

"But it wasn't fine," she whispered, still horrified, still deeply ashamed of what she'd done that day, and of how incredibly stupid and irresponsible she'd been. She had many highs and lows in her life, but that moment had been by far the lowest.

She fought a wave of nausea, her coffee and croissant perhaps not the best breakfast after all, and gripped the edge of the table, determined to keep her stomach from upending.

It didn't help that Colm was wrong.

He didn't know what he was saying. He didn't know what he was asking her to do. It was dangerous, so dangerous. Didn't he remember how broken she was? Didn't he realize she'd been cracked in two? Her skull fractured, bones snapped, lungs collapsed. "It's time to let me go, Colm."

"That's not going to happen."

"Colm, please."

"*Ever.*"

For a moment she couldn't breathe. For a moment everything just spun and her stomach heaved. She drew one short breath after another. "I know you're trying to do the right thing. But it's not the right thing, not if it hurts Jack."

"Ava, he's asking questions."

"Then answer them," she said huskily. "Tell him what

you've always told him—Mommy's sick. Mommy loves you but she can't take care of you."

The silence was thick and heavy, so heavy that Ava finally looked up at Colm. His blue-green gaze had lost all warmth, the depths now glacier cold.

"I'm not going to tell Jack that. I'm not going to lie to him."

"It's not a lie!"

"It is. Because you can take care of him. I *know* you can, and it's time you did."

She flinched, stung by his tone, but not entirely surprised. This was the tone he'd used with her at the beginning of her recovery. These were the same words, the same voice, the same relentless attitude. He wouldn't let her quit. Wouldn't accept her exhaustion or her tears of pain. Ignoring her protests, he crouched in front of her and strapped the braces on her legs, stood her up at the bars, and insisted she walk. *I know you,* he said, each time, every time, *I know you can do this.*

And that was how her rehab went. He coached her, pushed her, encouraged her, one day at a time. One foot in front of the other. Over and over and over.

Until the day he stopped coming.

The day he disappeared from her life was nearly as bad as the accident. The loss had hit her so hard, and she'd been so vulnerable, so physically and emotionally fragile.

"You're not being practical," she said lowly. "We have to

remember my limitations—"

"What crap!"

"It's true," she doggedly continued. "The doctors said—"

"They're wrong," he interrupted again, his voice rough with emotion. "They're wrong on this, Ava. I don't believe in limitations. And, dammit, neither do you." His voice dropped. "You can't, not when Jack needs you so much."

Her eyes closed at the shaft of pain. Jack had been her motivation. Jack had been the reason she could endure the grueling months of physical and speech therapy even after Colm stopped coming to see her.

She was determined she'd get her baby back. She'd be part of his life again. She so badly wanted to be a good mother. But her attempt to reconcile with two year old Jack had been a disaster. First, she'd scared him with her leg braces and walker, and then just when he'd come to terms with her disability, she'd taken him out in the stroller, she'd walked him to a shopping center…

And left him there.

Why?

What kind of woman did such a thing? What was wrong with her? What had she been thinking?

But in the end, the motivation didn't matter. The only thing that mattered was that she'd taken him from his home and abandoned him in a shopping center and then wandered away herself.

She was not a well woman. She was not to be trusted.

Ever.

"Then find him a good mother," Ava whispered, her voice flat, devoid of all emotion.

It'd been over a year since that awful day but she'd had thirteen months to examine her heart and the painful soul-searching had made her realize that Jack deserved better. Jack deserved a mother who could properly care for him. A mother who could run and play and make his life easier, not harder.

Colm broke the silence. "You don't mean that."

God, he knew her so well. Colm was right, of course. She didn't want anyone to take her place, didn't want to be replaced, and while she'd given up her braces and walker, there were still many things she found difficult to do.

"You can't give up," he added, after a moment, his deep voice sliding down her spine.

She ducked her head.

"You've made great strides, Ava. You've come back from the dead." He turned her chair, forcing her to face him.

There was something in his eyes and expression that seemed to strip her bare. She felt naked. Frightened. "I am not what I was before. Nor will I ever be her again."

He held her gaze, the bright blue depths scorching her. "So what do you want us to do? Bury you? Forget you? Act like you're dead?" He ground the words out, angry, and frustrated.

Ava could feel his tension, his energy palpable, practically pulsing within her, matching her heartbeat.

He swore. Violently. "Nothing is more important than our son."

"I will hurt him!"

"You will not. I won't let that happen." His gaze locked with hers, his features hard and fierce. "I promise you that, Ava."

He was a beautiful man, and angry, he looked intimidating. He was a Celtic warrior and he'd brought her to his kingdom, determined to conquer.

And he would conquer her, if she wasn't careful. He'd break her. There'd be nothing left of her when he was done.

"I love Jack, and yes, I would love to still be part of his life if I knew I wouldn't hurt him, but you…" She dragged in a breath, as angry with him as he was with her. "You are another story. You have no say over me. I will not allow you to dictate to me or trying to control me. Once, we were lovers, but that was a long, long time ago!"

Chapter Nine

S HE PUSHED AWAY from the table and took a panicked step backwards, bumping her chair hard enough to send pain shooting through her hip. Tears filled her eyes and she whimpered in protest.

Colm was on his feet, too, and she threw her hands up. "Don't touch me," she cried. "Don't come near me! I've had enough of you. I want to go. I want to return to the villa now."

"We're in the middle of the sea, Ava. We won't back at the villa until later this afternoon."

Her hip throbbed and her head had begun to ache. She rubbed at her temple, trying to ease the thumping, trying to calm down. Intense emotions brought on the headaches. She didn't need a migraine now.

Colm's brows pulled. He scrutinized her face. "Your head?"

"It'll be okay." She struggled to smile but couldn't.

He stretched a hand out to brush a fine dark tendril of

hair back from her brow, his fingers soothing against her temple. "Let's go find some shade. Get you something cool to drink. Do you need a tablet for the pain?"

She shook her head. "Let's just not argue anymore. I hate fighting with you."

"And I hate fighting with you. So let's change into our swim suits and relax, because, in another twenty minutes, we'll be anchoring at a spot where we'll swim and snorkel and see the most amazing fish."

Swimming and snorkeling proved to be the perfect distraction. Ava loved the water, and today she was the one begging to stay out and swim a little longer, and snorkel a little more. They splashed about for over an hour and then returned to the yacht for lunch, and then jumped back in for a second round of snorkeling.

Now they were sunbathing on the deck while the yacht ferried them to St. Barts' Lorient Bay.

Ava was lying on her back on a lounge chair, eyes closed, straw hat shading her eyes while she soaked up bright, hot rays. She was sleepy and relaxed, the kind of lazy pleasure one felt after exercising and taking in the sun. It'd been a week since she'd really exercised and she felt calmer than she had in days. She so enjoyed swimming. She needed to remember this.

"I wish I had my notebook," she said, breaking the companionable silence.

"What would you write down?" Colm asked, his deep

voice raspy. He, too, was drowsy from the sun.

She turned her head and peeked at him from beneath the brim of her hat. He was on a lounge chair just a foot away, filling it completely. He had a magnificent body. It all started with his height and those massive shoulders, and then there was that thickly muscled chest, the narrow waist and hips and long, strong legs. A work of art.

"I'd remind myself to swim more, and play more. I'd say that snorkeling today off your yacht was the most fun I've had in….oh, forever."

"We should do this more often."

"Snorkel?"

"And visit the villa. There's no reason we can't. We have the house. The plane. We just need to make the time."

Her lips curved. "Should I put that in the notebook, too?"

"Yes, please do." He reached over to her, and stroked her shoulder with a finger. "And write down that Colm loves you in your pale aqua bikini. That he thinks you are seriously sexy—"

"I'm not going to write that!" But she was laughing as she knocked his hand off her shoulder.

"Then I'm going to find your notebook and write it down. Or maybe I'll just start my own and then every day we can compare notes."

"Well, now I know what to get you for Christmas."

"Christmas is a long way off. Can we make it Valentine's

Day? That's coming up in just a couple weeks."

"If you remind me." She smiled impishly. "Every day." Snickering, she dragged the hat down low, shielding her eyes and stretched out, thinking it'd be nice to just doze off for a bit. But this time she couldn't relax. She couldn't get comfortable, now, when she was so aware of Colm lying on the lounge chair next to her, within reach.

He'd been so good with her today, such great company. He'd been engaging and charming, and attentive in the water, making sure she was always safe. And while she appreciated his concern, she enjoyed him most when he wasn't fussing over her, but focusing on her as a woman. Making her feel like a woman. A real woman. Whole, capable, attractive.

She understood that there were times they had to talk about her injury, but she didn't want every conversation to be about it. She had to be more than all the broken parts. Otherwise, what was the point?

She sensed Colm felt the same way, too. There were moments when they were together today where she just felt like Ava. Not the old Ava, or the new Ava, just Ava Galvan, and it felt good. It gave her hope.

Hope. She flexed her feet, then pointed, arching high in the instep, surreptitiously stretching her legs and toes, imagining herself on the dance floor, on pointe. Lovely, long taut muscles. Beautiful extension. A deep controlled breath—

And then in the next breath, she imagined herself beneath Colm, their skin warm and damp, his hands stroking her, making her wet. She missed him. She missed the way he could make her feel, and with her eyes closed, she could also imagine them together, his hips between her thighs, his body filling her, stretching her, making her feel good, making her feel beautiful.

She drew a shallow breath, in and out, so very conscious of him lying close to her now.

If she focused, she could remember how it had felt earlier today when he'd sat behind her, reapplying the sunscreen to her back. She'd felt almost delirious with pleasure as he swept the warm lotion into her skin, up and down in long luxurious strokes, working her shoulders and then down her back to where her spine dipped and a thousand nerves screamed for more.

He always made her feel so sensitive. Her body responded to him. It had been his way from the start.

She shifted on the lounge, trying to get comfortable but tension coiled low in her belly, an aching knot that ran straight up to her tender breasts, the nipples peaked inside her flimsy bikini top.

It was funny how sometimes conversation seemed to push them apart. All the words could leave her feeling confused and empty…disconnected…but the moment he touched her, the distance collapsed and all she wanted was him.

She wanted him now.

She'd been aware of him all afternoon, conscious of each gesture he made, each wry twist of his lips. She might forget what they talked about but she couldn't forget his kiss, or the pleasure of his touch and lying so close to him had made her almost dizzy with longing.

Colm turned over on his chair, looked at her. "You're getting restless."

"Yes."

"Bored?"

She didn't know how to tell him what she wanted. They weren't lovers anymore. Nor a couple. She couldn't just ask him to put his hands on her breasts and massage her ass and slide his fingers—

"Not bored," she choked, squeezing her legs together, feet flexing. She was hot and bothered in all the wrong ways and wanting relief, and he knew how to give her that release. He was shockingly talented in bed. He could make her climax a dozen different ways. And then there were his hands.

His mouth.

His long, hard, thick shaft…

And that tongue…soft, pointed, lapping, flicking…

She'd been convent educated the first eight years of her life and the nuns had been strict, teaching the girls that sex before marriage was a sin, and equally forbidden were sexual acts that didn't that permit procreation.

But there was nothing like Colm's mouth between her thighs, his tongue on her most sensitive flesh, licking. Sucking.

"So what are you thinking about?" he asked, rolling onto his side.

She glanced at him, grateful he couldn't read her mind, and yet, she couldn't read his either, not with the dark pair of sunglasses hiding his piercing gaze. "Argentina," she said huskily.

"Before the accident you rarely talked about your life back home. It's good to hear you talk about your childhood in Argentina. I know so little about your past."

She crossed her feet at her ankles, trying to ignore the hot ache within her.

"I've been in America since I was thirteen. New York is home. Buenos Aires feels like a dream."

"You don't miss it?"

"I miss my family, but we were not a close family. Over time, the ballet school became home and the dance company became my family."

"And you weren't ever homesick?"

"Oh, I was in the beginning. Terribly homesick. But I didn't tell anyone back home. I was afraid that if my parents knew how lonely I was, they would have brought me back to Buenos Aires, and yet dance was my passion. I knew that if I'd hoped to make it, to become one of the great ones, I had to train seriously, and properly. I got that training in New

York, with the Manhattan Ballet, and I was determined to stay there, even after they'd summoned me home."

"What do you mean, summoned?"

Her shoulders lifted and fell. "My father arranged a marriage for me when I was twenty. I refused to return home to marry Senor Carlito. My father was furious."

He barked a laugh. "An arranged marriage? For you?"

"Yes, obviously my father did not know me well. He hadn't anticipated my refusal, either, confident he'd overcome my objections." She shot him a rueful glance as she struggled to sit up. "Confident enough that the wedding invitations were mailed, and the dress ordered. Imagine his fury and shame when my mother had to send a second set of cards in the mail informing the five hundred guests that there would be no wedding."

"I have a feeling he might be the type to hold a grudge."

"Oh, most definitely. My father stopped communicating with me. He may have disowned me. It's just as well if he did, he wouldn't want me the way I am now."

Colm sat up swiftly. "And how are you now?"

She shrugged, grimaced. "Let's not play this game."

"It's not a game."

"Then you know how I am. I'm damaged. A woman with half a brain."

He took his sunglasses off, tossing them onto the foot of the lounger. "Your brain is all there."

"But I'm slower. You know I am."

"You're also alive. And I think you're amazing. You're the one who is hard on you. Not me."

"I know the kind of woman you like—"

"You're the woman I like, and you are the only woman I want." He reached over and lifted her from her chair to settle her onto his lap. "The only one," he repeated, cupping the back of her head, bringing her face to his. He kissed her slowly, deeply, his tongue probing her mouth, making her squirm.

The kiss was good but not enough. She wanted more heat, wanted fire. Wanted tension and passion and the feel of him driving into her, filling her, blocking every thought and sensation.

His hand tangled in her hair, twining the strands around his palm. He pulled hard enough to make her gasp and he bit into her soft lip. She gasped again, shifting forward on his lap, needing friction.

"Mine," he ground out, nipping again at her lip even as his fingers found one taut nipple. He played with the tip, rolling it, palming it, before pinching. She saw stars, and rocked against him, hot, wet. He soothed where he'd inflicted pain, rubbing, strumming before pinching the tender nipple again. "You are mine."

His hands were now at her waist, and then sliding over her hips, pushing away the flimsy sarong to run his hands up her thighs, and down again to her knees and then trailing them back up the inside of her thighs.

She shivered as he parted her legs, widening them and pushing her more firmly onto his lap, making her aware of his erection. He was very hard and very warm and she could feel the thick rounded head of his shaft against her, pressing right where she was most sensitive.

Holding her hips he rocked her over his shaft, dragging her back and forth until she was grabbing at his shoulders, fighting to stay put, wanting the head of his shaft in her, not against her.

Colm wasn't having it. He was in charge, he was controlling this and he caught her hands in one of his, locking them behind her back. She felt fully exposed, her breasts thrusting out, her legs parted, her body his to touch, to tease, to claim.

"Whose are you?" he murmured, tugging her hands back an inch so her back arched and her neck was exposed. His lips brushed her skin, light kisses that made her head spin.

She felt wild for him. Desperate for relief. She dragged in air but couldn't speak.

His mouth was at her collarbone, and then kissing his way down the slope of a breast before covering the pebbled nipple. He worked the nipple through the silky fabric, a rhythmic sucking that made her womb contract. He was making her so hot and wet. Too hot and wet.

"Touch me," she begged.

"Only if you tell me who you are."

"Ava."

"And what are you?"

She groaned as his hand found her between her thighs, cupping her damp heat. "Yours."

"Yes, mine. My woman. My lover. My pleasure."

She nearly swooned as his palm pressed up against her, the heat of his hand scalding. She might as well have been naked. Her bikini bottoms provided no protection.

He palmed her mound, finding her nub. She shuddered against him.

"Look at me," he commanded.

She couldn't. She felt too exposed, too wanton.

"Look at me," he repeated, his teeth catching at the curve of her ear, biting lightly and then harder on the lobe.

She shuddered at the twin rivulets of sensation—pleasure and pain—but the lasting sensation was pleasure. It felt good. Too good. He knew her so well.

She opened her eyes, her gaze locking with his. His eyes were dark with desire, the color of the sea, but bright and fierce. He wanted her. It was a heady thought, and so very dangerous because a little bit with him was never enough. She always wanted more.

"We can't do this here, Colm," she said huskily.

"Why not?" he challenged, finding her through the bottoms, lightly tracing the lines of her, the curves, the softness, the seams.

She shivered as he skimmed from her lips to the ridge of her clit, his fingertip lingering on the sensitive bud, circling, teasing.

He kissed her to silence her groan, then murmured against her mouth, "I am going to make you come here."

"Not here," she begged, even as she bucked helplessly against his hand.

"Then where?" His hand eased beneath the edge of the bottoms, slipping under fabric to find hot, slick skin.

"Don't know, don't care." She gasped, as he caressed her folds and then slipped a finger between.

And all she wanted was more.

More pressure, more friction, more satisfaction.

He pressed deeper and she groaned as he touched a sensitive spot inside of her. Her knees shook and she arched.

"Take me to your room," she begged. "You can have me, all of me, just take me somewhere private. Please?"

Chapter Ten

WITH VIRTUALLY NOTHING on, it took no time to strip bare, and with all the touching and kissing outside on the sundeck, Ava didn't want any more foreplay. She wanted Colm, buried deep inside of her. He might be gifted with talented fingers and lips and a tongue but nothing in the world felt as good as him filling her, his body covering hers, his skin warming her from the inside out.

With hands linked and bodies as one, she felt beautiful and powerful.

She felt hope and possibility. Safety and security.

She felt love. Oh, she loved him. She'd always loved him. And when they were together like this, she knew she'd always love him. It was impossible not to. She was his, and he was hers and she didn't know why she'd spent the past thirteen months trying to forget him. She'd never be over him. She'd never not want him.

They made love once, and then again, and it wasn't until much later when they were lying in bed, sleepy and sated, that Ava, curled against Colm, her cheek on his chest, found the courage to ask the thing that troubled her most.

"Jack," she whispered. "Is he…okay? Is he healthy? Happy?"

Colm stroked her long hair, smoothing it down her back. "Yes. He's perfect."

Ave felt a prick of pain and she blinked, holding back tears as she pictured the dark-eyed toddler she'd last seen thirteen months ago. She didn't remember much from that visit, just the sense that he'd been active, busy, and into absolutely everything. "He really is normal?"

"He's a very smart little boy. Off the charts, actually. Our son is apparently gifted."

She looked up at Colm, trying to see his face in the deepening shadows filling the room. "How do you know?"

"He has an ear for music. He doesn't yet read sheet music, but if he hears a piece, he can pick it out, find the keys. I've just started him with a piano teacher and he loves it. His teacher said he's never met another child with so much passion." Colm dipped his head and pressed a kiss to her temple. "I'm not surprised, though. He's your son. Of course he's gifted. He has your fire and passion."

Her eyes welled up quickly. She couldn't stop a tear from falling onto Colm's chest. She missed him. Her baby.

Another tear fell.

And then another.

She couldn't stop them anymore.

"So I didn't hurt him?" She choked. "He really is okay."

"He's better than okay. He's sweet and kind and smart and lovely in every way. I look at him and see you. He is truly your son—"

"Our son," she interrupted.

"Our son," he agreed quietly. "And he is blessed. Except for missing you. He does miss you, Ava. Terribly."

She flinched. "He doesn't know me."

"He keeps your picture by his bed."

"I would think he hates me—"

"He doesn't remember anything bad. He doesn't re-member you leaving him. He only knows that you love him, and have been ill, and he prays every night that you will soon be well so that you can come be his mommy again."

"*Stop.*"

"I'm telling you the truth."

Her heart fell even as her stomach cramped. She squeezed her eyes shut to keep fresh tears from falling. The anguish was real, and intense. Jack, her baby, who was never breastfed. Her baby that was never rocked by her, held by her, never walked by her as he wailed in the middle of the night, hungry. Lonely. Inconsolable.

She was almost sobbing and she couldn't catch her breath.

For the last year and a half she'd tried to tell herself Jack would be fine. She tried to tell herself that he wouldn't miss her, he wouldn't need her, that Colm would find a beautiful, young wife and Jack would finally have the mother he needed. The mother he *needed*. The mother she couldn't be.

Colm's arms circled her and she cried against him, grieving for all she'd lost, and the years she couldn't get back.

Was it too late to be his mother?

Was it too late to try again?

As her tears subsided, Colm kissed the top of her head. "If you had your notebook here, what would you write in it, right now?" he asked her quietly.

She drew a shuddering breath. "That I love him. I love Jack. And I'd give anything to be his mom again."

He kissed her again. "He needs you, Ava."

"And I need him."

AVA WOKE TO the gentle rocking of the boat. It took her several long moments to sort out where she was, and it was only because Colm reached for her, drawing her back to him that she remembered.

His yacht.

His bed.

His arms.

"Are you okay?" he asked, his deep voice a rumble in the dark bedroom.

"Yes." But why was her throat raw? Why did everything feel broken inside of her? "No." She pressed herself to Colm, her legs between his, her face against his chest. "I am sad. Why am I sad?"

"We talked about Jack tonight. You cried because you miss him."

Her eyes welled with tears. "He doesn't know me. I am a stranger to him."

"He is so young. He has an entire life ahead of him. You can be part of that life. It's not too late. You've never been stronger, or healthier—"

"I still forget things though. My short term memory is terrible." She pushed up on her elbow. "And I want Jack, but I don't just want Jack. I want you. I need you."

He caught her face and kissed her lips. "I know, baby. I need you, too. It's time to come home. Time for us to be together again, a family again. You know you want to. And you know it's the right thing to do."

WHEN SHE WOKE up again it was morning, sunlight pouring through the slats at the window.

Colm wasn't in bed but she found him in the connecting bathroom's shower.

She opened the glass door and stepped into the shower, dissipating the steam. "Well, hello there," he said, drawing her under the hot water spray. "Have you come for a shampoo and wash?"

"I'm not sure," she answered. "I heard the shower and thought I should come see what all the fuss was about."

He took her hand and wrapped it around his hard length. "This is the situation," he said, his hand covering hers as they firmly stroked him. He grew even thicker and harder beneath her touch.

Her eyes widened as her gaze locked with his. "Impressive."

"It wants you, baby. But I'm worried after yesterday you might be sore."

She didn't know about sore. It was hard to think about being sore when his free hand was playing with her body, soaping her breasts, kneading the nipples. She arched and he stroked down her belly to slide fingers between her curls to find her clit.

She stroked him harder.

His fingers were between her legs, and then slipping into her. She groaned and then nearly fell when he went down in the shower onto his knees and hooked one of her legs over his shoulder, put his mouth on her and took her with his tongue.

She came hard, but he wasn't done, and turning her around he slowly entered her from behind, filling her slick, tight core until she'd taken all of his length.

With him buried deeply, he caressed the length of her, finding her breasts, the small of her waist, the curve of her hips. He didn't move or thrust and yet with him seated so deeply within her, she began to pulse around him, and the more her body squeezed him, the more he filled her and it was mind-blowing being so still and yet feeling so much.

"Don't come," he murmured, pressing his fingers to her

clit while her body gripped his length, contracting internally.

He was hot, she was hot, she felt as if she was going to explode. It was so damn erotic. He was so damn erotic.

"Don't come," he repeated, parting her folds, opening the soft swollen lips to expose her to the air.

"I need to come." She couldn't think, couldn't breathe, her body throbbing, her nerves taut, skin tingling. "Touch me and let me come."

"You want this."

"Yes."

"You need this."

"Yes."

"You need me."

"Yes. Always."

And then he touched her and she shattered, like the fireworks on the fourth of July. Her orgasm triggered his and they came together and, as she leaned against the shower wall, it struck her that although the sex was incredibly good and incredibly hot, they'd never once mentioned the word love.

But then, she shouldn't be surprised. He'd never loved her. Why should she think it'd be different now?

BREAKFAST WAS SERVED on the sundeck at a table set for two. Neither Ava nor Colm were very talkative during the meal. She didn't mind. She was definitely languid from the night of lovemaking.

Between sips of coffee, she pulled her warm, chocolate-filled croissant apart, popping bites into her mouth.

It was a beautiful morning. The sun reflected brightly off the water, the sea sparkling all around them.

It was an almost perfect morning.

It was an almost perfect holiday.

She was almost satisfied. Physically she was sated. Colm was a skilled and generous lover. He always made sure he took care of her before he asked for anything himself. She appreciated his skill. Her body hummed from all the attention but she hated how her heart felt empty.

Colm had talked about her moving in with him. He'd talked about them becoming a family for Jack. But if Ava was honest, she wasn't sure she could handle spending her life with someone who didn't love her.

She needed to tell him somehow. She needed to let him know that they couldn't just move forward with plans…at least, not with his plans. Surely, there was a way to see Jack and still protect her heart?

"Should we talk about what happens next?" Colm asked, breaking the silence.

Her insides suddenly felt fluttery, as if she'd swallowed a handful of butterflies. "Okay."

His eyes narrowed a fraction. "You don't sound very enthusiastic."

"It's scary."

"I thought you wanted to give Jack a family. I thought

you wanted to be with him."

She wasn't sure how to answer that. Because, yes, she wanted Jack loved and happy, but she worried that she wouldn't be loved and happy living with Colm. "I'm just wondering if there are options we haven't explored."

"What do you mean?"

"Maybe we should try to work me into Jack's life slowly with visits…playtime…things like that."

"You don't want to live with him?"

"I do, but I'm not sure it would be good for him if I live with you."

Colm just stared at her, expression shuttered, and, as the silence stretched, it became heavier and more uncomfortable.

"I'm confused," he said after a long moment. "I thought—" He broke off, brow furrowing, his jaw tightening. "What about us?"

She swallowed hard and wrapped her fingers around the stem of her water glass. "There isn't an us, though."

"Ava."

"We're good in bed. But that's all we are, all we have."

"Oh, Ava."

"You know it's true. You never wanted me. You didn't want Jack, either—"

"That's the past. We have to leave that in the past. It's time we lived in the present. We have a son who is three and he needs his parents to pull together, to function together. And we can. We can be a real family. It's what you wanted for Jack. It's what I want for Jack. It's the best thing for him. We both know that."

No wonder Colm had been so successful in life. He made everything sound easy. He didn't believe in complications. He ignored obstacles. But she wasn't like that.

She couldn't bury her head in the sand. "One doesn't just create a stable family, Colm. Stability comes from within. It can't be imposed from the outside."

"It won't be imposed. It's something we're choosing. And it's the right decision."

She didn't speak, struggling to organize her thoughts, trying to make sense of the objections forming inside of her. She knew he was right about Jack needing security and stability but Ava knew she needed the same thing. She didn't do well with chaos. She needed calm, and structure and order.

In the silence, she could hear a voice from a steward down below, and the lap of waves against the side of the sleek yacht.

"What you're suggesting is practically an arranged marriage," she said finally.

"But I didn't want to marry Senor Carlito, and I don't want to marry you. Not if you don't love me. That's why you were so upset about the pregnancy. You didn't love me and didn't want a baby with me. You were angry because you felt like I was trapping you."

One brow lifted. "Weren't you?"

Her jaw dropped, shocked. "You really did feel that way?"

"I'd be lying to you if I told you it hadn't crossed my mind."

"Why would I trap you?"

He shrugged. "You loved me. You didn't feel secure about my affections. It was a way to keep me in your life."

Sickened, Ava stumbled to her feet. Pushing away from the table, she walked as quickly as she could from the sun deck, her hand on the rail for support.

Beneath her feet the yacht shifted, rolling. They were moving again. She could hear waves breaking against the bow.

"Ava, stop," Colm called after her, following.

"Leave me alone." She choked, hating him, hating how he ruined everything. The pleasure he gave her never equaled the pain he caused her.

His footsteps sounded behind her and then his hand closed around her arm, forcing her to a stop. "Stop running from me. You're going to hurt yourself."

"Better I hurt myself then let you hurt me with more of your words!" She flashed, bruised. "How little you thought of me…how much you must despise me to imagine I'd trap you with an unplanned pregnancy."

"You weren't always so ethical," he said, pinning her with his body against the railing. "You're an intelligent, passionate woman. But that doesn't make you a saint."

He was leaning close, far too close. She could smell his spice and vanilla fragrance, the scent heightened by the heat of the sun and the warmth of his skin and her whole body reacted, nerves screaming. "I've always been ethical," she protested. "I'm a product of convent education. I know my ten commandments better than anyone."

"Then you know, thou shalt not lie."

"I'm not lying. I've no need to lie. Ask me what you want to know and I'll tell you…if I can remember."

His head dipped, his mouth grazed the corner of hers, placing the lightest kiss possible on the edge of her lips. "How convenient."

His whisper sent icy-hot rivulets of feeling up and down her spine while his light kiss made her tummy curl and the hair rise on her nape. She remembered the way he'd kissed her in the shower, remembered the heat and intense sensation.

She shook her head, chasing the memories away. "At least I was willing to give you my heart! You wouldn't even offer me that."

His blue-green gaze sparked. "I did care for you. But it wasn't enough for you."

Care, she repeated silently. What a small strange word. Completely colorless, nearly sterile. Like caregiver and caretaker and everything else cold and burdensome. Care and duty could be sisters. Dowdy sisters while love, joy, and pleasure were the beauties that went to the ball.

"No." She gritted. "You're right. I wanted more than that. I wanted love. I wanted you. I wanted forever."

"And now you have it." And his head came down, his mouth taking hers in a hard, punishing kiss.

He kissed her until she clung to him, unable to stand without his support. He kissed her until she was dazed and breathless and unable to argue.

"You have it," he repeated. "My wife."

Chapter Eleven

*W*IFE?

 She blinked at him, still dazed, and very confused. "What did you say?"

"Wife." The corner of his mouth lifted. "You're my wife, Ava. We're already married. We've been married since last Thanksgiving."

"That's not true."

He pulled Ava from the breezy deck, through doors, into a pretty sitting room. "It most certainly is. For richer or poorer, in sickness and in health," he said.

She sank into the nearest chair, her legs no longer able to support her. "I don't believe you."

Colm drew a slim leather wallet from his pocket and opened it to show her a photo he kept next to his driver's license.

It was a picture of a bride and groom and the groom was holding a toddler in a black suit. "This is us fourteen months ago. This is our family. You, me, and Jack, on the day of our wedding."

Ava studied the photo intently. Handsome Colm in a tuxedo. Baby Jack in an almost identical suit. And her in a white, formfitting gown. She was holding flowers. She was smiling. They were all smiling.

She looked up at Colm. "I see the picture but I don't remember."

"The point is, we are married already. We are a family. Jack has a family. It's time we moved forward, not back."

She couldn't tear her gaze from the photo. "Why don't I remember?"

"You took Jack out in his stroller four days after the ceremony. You left him there and walked away. By the time the police found you, you didn't remember any of it. The doctors thought you might regain some of your memories if given time, and I think you did regain many memories, but you never regained all."

"And you've been waiting all these months for me to remember?"

"You're my wife, Ava. I will wait the rest of my life for you. But what about Jack? Is it right, or fair, to make him wait?"

Her heart thumped. She felt wild on the inside but she couldn't lose it. She had to stay calm, because Colm was right. Jack deserved more. Jack deserved better. "So how do we do this? What happens now?"

"We get our son and we bring him home."

THEY REACHED LORIENT Bay just before noon and as the crew dropped anchor, a motorboat sped from the beach to come pick Colm and Ava up.

Ava's heart pounded as she watched the motorboat race towards them. She was nervous, and afraid. She turned to look at Colm, who was standing next to her. "How will this work?" she asked softly. "I don't even know where you and Jack live. Are you still in Palm Beach?"

"I sold that house. Was kind of short on good memories there, seemed better to just get rid of it." Colm's gaze met hers. "Jack and I live in Manhattan."

Her eyes widened. "I had no idea. Where in Manhattan?"

"Carnegie Hill."

"That's a very nice neighborhood."

"It's a very nice house, too. You'll like it."

He was so sure of himself. She envied his confidence. She wasn't sure of anything anymore. "And Jack? When will I see him?"

"Soon." He smiled at her. "Don't be nervous. There's no reason to be nervous. Everything is going to be fine."

"Even though I don't feel like your wife?" She countered with an unsteady smile.

He gave her a thoughtful look. "I guess that would be a problem. What we need is a wedding. It shouldn't be a problem. We can put that together in a just a few days."

"Colm."

"Don't worry about a thing. Just leave all the arrangements to me."

The speed boat slowed, and deckhands went into action, lowering a ladder and tying the small speedboat to the side of the yacht so Colm and Ava could disembark.

The boat swayed as Ava stepped down and she nearly fell. Colm caught her elbow, steadying her.

She thanked him and sat down. Colm took a seat across from her.

Her head was spinning. She was struggling to process the past twenty-four hours. It wasn't easy to make sense of everything they'd done, and everything he'd told her.

"We really are married," she said.

He nodded.

"Was it a big wedding?"

"No."

"It was a very small wedding. A civil ceremony at the Palm Beach courthouse."

"Why did we marry that way?"

"You didn't want fuss."

"Maybe that's why I don't remember it. There wasn't enough fuss." She met his gaze, grimaced. "Sorry. That was supposed to be a joke."

"It was funny."

She made a soft, rough sound. "I don't think there is any point in marrying again. If we are married, and if we never divorced, why go through all those hoops?"

"Maybe this time you'll remember."

"But knowing my track record, probably not."

"I guess we're going to be having a lot of weddings then." He laughed at her stricken expression. "It's okay. We don't have to tell anyone. It'll be our own private thing."

She laughed, because it was that or cry.

THE SPEED BOAT slowed close to shore, and the driver pulled the motor up and then got them a little bit closer, making it easy for Colm to step out without getting too wet and carry Ava onto dry sand.

They walked along the beach, towards the gondola platform, and in the distance Ava spotted a woman seated on a towel with a small child building a sand castle.

Jack could be that age, she thought, watching the little boy dig with his shovel, his shoulders small but sturdy, his head bent in concentration.

She glanced at Colm, saw he was watching the mother and child, too. "They're lovely, aren't they?" Ava asked, feeling the old ache whenever she thought of Jack.

"Very."

She stopped, shielded her eyes to watch the pair on the sand and Colm stood with her. "I didn't trap you," she said quietly. "The pregnancy was an accident, but once I found out about Jack, I wanted him. Badly." Her heart felt tender, almost bruised. "I still want him. But I just don't want to hurt him. Not ever again. And I trust you, Colm. I trust you to make sure it won't happen."

"You have my word."

"Because I'd never forgive myself if something happened to him again. I couldn't hand it. I still hate myself for what happened last year, because I know he's a miracle. He survived my accident, and my coma, and being born months too early. He's a gift. I know that. Which is why I can't let him be hurt—"

"*Ava.*" Colm swore softly and reached for her. He held her against him, his fingers sliding through her hair. "It's going to be okay. We'll make this work. We will."

"But what if I hurt him again?"

"You won't."

"How do you know?"

"Because I have faith, and I believe we can do this. Together." His blue-green eyes blazed, his expression fierce and determined. "We can."

Before she could answer, a high jubilant voice shouted, "Daddy! Daddy! You're home!"

Turning, Ava saw the little boy in the bright yellow and blue swim trunks sprint across the beach, small feet kicking up the sand. He had big, dark eyes, olive skin, and he was laughing, delighted by the appearance of his father.

"Jack?" she whispered, a hand against her heart.

He looked achingly familiar. Just a wisp of a boy with dark hair that could use a cut. A ringlet lay on his forehead and as he ran, he reached up, and ruffled his hair, disturbing the curl.

As Colm swung Jack into his arms, Ava realized that Jack looked just like her brother, Tadeo. It was a bittersweet resemblance. Tadeo had died young, just a year after Ava moved to New York.

"Introduce me, Colm," she said, voice husky.

But Jack didn't need an introduction. He lifted his dark head from his father's shoulder and stared at Ava for a long, somber moment before whispering, "You're my Mommy."

Ava felt an explosion of pain, the emotion almost unbearable. "Yes," she answered, reaching out to gently touch Jack's dark hair. He was beautiful. Still so young. Half-baby, half-boy, she could see the tenderness in him, the softness at the edges of his mouth and jaw and chin.

Jack caught her fingers in his hand and he held them tight. "You came home."

"Yes."

"Where were you?" he asked.

She blinked, swallowed the huge lump filling her throat. "Lost."

His eyes had filled with tears, too. "But Daddy found you."

Chapter Twelve

D ID ALL BRIDES feel this nervous?

Ava smoothed her ivory and gold couture gown over her tummy, feeling the butterflies grow by the minute. She shouldn't be so nervous. Colm had said it wouldn't be a fussy wedding, but moving to her bedroom window she peered through the slats of the plantation shutter and saw the stream of elegant couples heading towards the party tents.

Society wedding.

The words flashed through her mind as she let the shutter close. In less than a half hour she was marrying Colm McKenzie, international tycoon, doting father…sensual lover.

Her cheeks flamed and she felt heat burst to life in her middle, radiating in hot rays of awareness throughout her limbs.

A knock sounded on her door and the door opened. It was Colm.

His thick, dark blonde hair had been combed earlier but

he must have ruffled it with an impatient hand and bits stood up at the front.

She went to him and smoothed the front down. "It was a little rock and roll," she said, smiling at him. "But it did call attention to your cheekbones."

"I do have fabulous cheekbones."

She laughed out loud. "You're mad."

"For you."

She shook her head, silently contradicting him.

"Yes. It's true." His lips curved in a slow appreciative smile. "And tonight you look simply stunning. You look like a princess. A Spanish princess."

She smiled ruefully. "My father is a count."

"And your mother must have been a goddess."

"I'm serious."

"I'm sure you are. You're always serious these days." He was teasing her but his eyes were brilliant and intent, and she felt his hunger for her. If nothing else, she knew he desired her.

Reaching her side, Colm drew a small jeweler's box from inside his tuxedo pocket and snapped it open to reveal a sparkling marquis-cut diamond set in platinum. "Your engagement ring," he said, taking her left hand and slipping the ring onto her fourth finger.

"Is this really mine?"

"It is yours. I've been keeping it for you this last year."

"I am so ashamed I don't remember—"

"No shame," he murmured, kissing her, silencing her. "We go forward, not back. There is no living in the past. We celebrate today. And that's what we will do every day."

Her eyes welled with tears and Ava held her ring up to the light. She turned her hand this way and that, transfixed by the stone's radiance. "Look how it sparkles."

"It's the way it was cut," he said, watching her face, not the ring. "The hard cuts reveal the diamond's true beauty. Like you," he added, kissing her once more, his lips lingering, making her tummy a crazy somersault.

Ava drew a breath, dragging in air, light-headed all over again. "Thank you."

Their eyes met and held. She loved the beautiful blue-green of his eyes, so vivid, so intense. So him.

"You've always been beautiful, Ava, but the accident revealed your true spirit. You are courageous. A fighter. And a wonderful role model for our son."

She felt a flicker of feeling in her heart, a tingling much like she'd felt during her rehab as she forced the muscles to life again. "Jack seems happy, doesn't he?"

"He's ecstatic. He adores you. Adores every minute with you."

"Just as I adore being with him."

"Have you noticed how much he likes to help you remember things? His pictures…his notes…?"

"I have. His nanny is so good, too. She never makes me feel like a third wheel."

"She is good," he agreed. "But from the beginning she knew the goal was to reunite you and Jack. And she's talked to Jack about you and helped create memories for him, of you."

"And then you've put all these scraps and notes and photos in a book for me." Her heart was on fire but in a good way. It was full of love, full of gratitude. "You've given me a life. You've made all this possible—"

"Don't cry." He caressed her cheek. "This is a happy day."

"I know. I'm just so thankful. Just so grateful, as I realize we might be able to make this work."

"Then come with me. I have one more thing to show you. I was going to save it for after the wedding but I want you to see it now." He led her from her bedroom, down the hall, to his room. They'd waited to share the master bedroom until after tonight's ceremony. The master bedroom was full of flowers and candles but that was not what Colm wanted her to see. He led Ava to a pair of chairs by the French doors and on one of the chairs was a big ivory leather scrapbook topped with a silver bow.

"For you," he said.

She sat down in the chair and took the bow off the oversized leather album. A small gold plaque was centered in the middle of the soft ivory leather.

The Story of Us

She looked up at Colm. "Did you make this for me?"

His lips curved, his smile crooked. "Open it."

She did, and as she flipped through the pages, her eyes filled with tears. He'd taken photos from the week and a half here in St. Barts and added things she'd said, her feelings and memories, as well as Jack's pictures and drawings. The big book covered just a week and a half of her life and yet it was full of beautiful sunrises and sunsets and smiles and love.

It was filled with love.

She could feel it. See it. Read it. Touch it. Maybe he didn't say the words, *I love you*, but they were in every page of this book. In every one of his actions.

He crouched next to her and wiped her tears, one by one. "Why are you crying? This was supposed to make you happy."

"It does."

"You're practically sobbing, baby."

"I know. And I'm ruining my makeup."

"Then why the tears?"

She looked up at him, her heart so full she couldn't contain it all. "I just realized that you really do care for me. You do."

He carefully caught more tears, swiping gently beneath her eyes. "Of course I do."

"I wasn't sure. I didn't think—"

"Ava, I love you."

"Because I'm Jack's mom?"

"Because you are extraordinary. You are Ava Galvan. The love of my life."

She drew a shuddering breath. "Promise?"

"Yes."

"Will you put that in the book?"

"Darling, it already is." And he turned the pages to one of the last pages that had been filled and there was a photo of him and her, the selfie taken on the beach the night they'd dined in the cabana. His arms were around her and they were laughing up at the camera together. Beneath the photo he'd written:

I love you, Ava, more than the stars in the sky and the water in the sea.

She touched the words, over and over. He did love her. He did. Even though she was broken and damaged and not the great ballerina…

He loved her anyway.

He loved her for her.

She looked up at him, eyes welling with tears all over again. "I love you."

"I know. And I thank you, Ava, for teaching me what love is."

COLM HAD SAID they were having a wedding overlooking the beach and she'd imagined something pretty and simple, but she should have known nothing Colm planned would be ordinary.

Reaching the garden Ava entered a magical world of gold lanterns and ropes of garland. Two enormous party tents glowed with soft yellow light but these were still empty as all the guests were gathered before a cupola formed from bare branches, decorated with thousands of cream and yellow orchids and roses.

They were waiting for her. As Ava paused and drew a quick breath, she heard the music change, the tempo becoming lighter, faster. She spotted Colm beneath the canopy of orchids and roses and all the knots in her middle dissolved. Yes. Everything was going to be fine.

Everything would be new, and challenging, but most of all, exciting.

The ceremony wasn't particularly long, but the vows were sincere and heartfelt. Ava felt Jack's rapt gaze as she and Colm exchanged rings and turning her head, she caught sight of Jack dressed in a black tuxedo, still clutching the ring pillow. His dark eyes were wide, his expression serious. He knew this was a monumental occasion.

He was, she thought, the heart and soul of the future.

Reaching out, she drew him forward, and held his hand in hers as the priest blessed them. This wasn't just a wedding, this was a homecoming, and Jack belonged in the warm protective circle with them.

When the elegant candlelit ceremony ended, the real party began. Dinner was interrupted repeatedly by toasts and warm wishes from Colm's friends and Colm himself was eager to celebrate. He started the dancing early by leading a laughing Ava to the empty dance floor. "I can't do this…I can't dance anymore."

"No can'ts. Don't believe in them. Won't accept them."

She laughed, half-embarrassed, half-amused. But as the band struck up their song, and he took her right hand in his and placed his hand low on her hip, she felt a tremor of trepidation. Ava drew a slow, shuddering breath to calm herself. "I'm not much of a dancer anymore."

"I've never been much of a dancer, so that makes us even."

"You used to love to dance. Way back when."

"Only because I loved dancing with you." His fingers curled around hers and he drew her right hand to his chest. She felt the steady beat of his heart beneath her palm. "I haven't danced in years. Not since you were hurt."

The music was playing but they were hardly moving, oblivious to the guests.

"We didn't dance at our last wedding?"

"No. It was a courthouse ceremony. Nothing like this. No party or reception."

She glanced to her right, watching guests fill the dance floor. "Who are these people? Where did you find them?"

He laughed. "The Caribbean is full of New Yorkers trying to escape the cold this time of year. It wasn't hard to round up a few friends."

"You went to so much trouble."

"I wanted to celebrate our marriage. I wanted to celebrate you."

Her chest squeezed tight, constricting air. "It's...crazy. But wonderful. I am just worried I won't remember all of this."

"Then I'll do it again and again. In fact, maybe every year on our anniversary we'll have a big wedding and party—"

"That's a terrible waste of money."

"Not if it gives you pleasure, and lets me show you how much I love you."

She couldn't speak. Her head felt light. "I still can't believe you really do love me."

His eyes, more green than blue tonight, shone down at her and he stroked her flushed cheek. "Ava, why else would I have married you? I love you more than any man has ever loved a woman."

The slow song had ended but she didn't move. It was impossible to move, much less think when her heart was beating so hard it threatened to burst free from her rib cage.

He loved her. He loved her for her and they both loved Jack and she'd always loved Colm...it was too much. She couldn't quite take it all in. Was the happy ending really hers? Was her most secret wish finally coming true?

"Malcolm." A woman joined them on the dance floor. She was slender and wore an elegant black sheath and matching coat.

Colm stiffened. Ava felt him tense. "Eden."

The woman's dark blonde hair was twisted in a sleek, French chignon and tiny lines creased at her eyes but they did nothing to diminish her beauty. "You're back then?"

His brows pulled. "I never left."

"You went to New York for a couple of years."

"I have a place in Manhattan but I never let the house go. I just closed it for a couple years."

Eden's jaw tightened. "I see."

As if suddenly remembering Ava, Colm drew her closer to his side. "Eden, this is Ava. Ava, Eden—"

"The ex-wife," Eden finished coolly.

Chapter Thirteen

X-WIFE? AVA stiffened, her insides freezing. Colm had been married before? Was that something he'd told her and she'd forgotten…or had he never told her…?

She tried to pull away but Colm kept his arm firmly around her waist.

"What are you doing here?" Colm asked Eden, his voice pitched low.

Eden's lips compressed, the fine lines at her eyes deepening. "I had to come. I had to see for myself."

"You weren't invited."

"Half the island was invited. I don't see what the problem was." Eden turned to look at Ava, her expression dismissive before turning her attention back to Malcolm. "Is it true you have a son?"

Ava shivered. Colm hugged her more firmly to his side. "Yes," he answered shortly. "Jack."

Eden let out a laugh but it sounded too high, too strained. "We never started a family. I didn't think Colm wanted a family." She paused, and smiled at Colm, her eyes glittering with pain and rage. "Obviously, it was just not with me."

"Eden, you need to leave."

Eden glanced at Ava. "He'll get rid of you, too. He will. It's just a matter of time."

"That's enough, Eden." Colm gestured and one of his wait staff appeared. "Please see Ms. Vail out," he instructed his staff.

"It's Mrs. McKenzie," Eden corrected. "McKenzie. Your wife."

Colm didn't respond. He turned away, and walked Ava off the dance floor.

Ava was shaking. Her thoughts rushed in a dozen different directions, the intense emotion making it difficult to think clearly. It was shocking, so shocking.

Ava shivered as they walked, chilled to the bone.

"She doesn't know what she's saying." Colm said, breaking the tense silence.

Ava swallowed around the bitterness in her mouth. "You never told me you were married before…or maybe you did, and I just don't remember."

"I didn't tell you."

"Why?"

His broad shoulders shrugged. "It's a period of my life I don't focus on."

"Yes, but it'd would have been good to know. I would

have liked to know that there had been a first Mrs. Malcolm McKenzie."

"That's ridiculous. It changes nothing."

"It does for me!"

He'd lead her from the party, through the garden to the master suite. The candles had ben lit. Champagne chilled in a silver bucket of ice. The bouquets of fresh flowers glowed in the soft light.

"Why does it matter?" he asked her, closing the bedroom door behind them.

"It just does…it's something I would want to know. It's something I ought to know."

"Why? It doesn't have any bearing on you and me. It's not part of the story of us—"

"But it's the story of you. And I realize I don't know anything about you."

"Not true," he said, loosening his bow tie. "You know I love you, and have fought for you and have fought for our future—"

"Why did you divorce her?" She interrupted, heart aching, eyes gritty with tears she didn't want to cry.

"It's complicated."

"You don't think I could handle it?"

"*No*." Colm shed his tuxedo jacket. "It's complicated because I don't even understand. We married a number of years before I met you. The marriage lasted less than a year. She was terribly unhappy and *she* left me. She ran off with a friend of mine. And that ended badly, too."

"But she said—"

"She's not well," he interrupted wearily. "She's never been well. I just didn't know it then."

"But you must have loved her because you married her."

"She was pregnant," he said bluntly. "Or so she said. And I married her because it was the right thing to do."

Ava sat down on the foot of the bed. "I'm sorry. I'm not following this very well."

"She told me she was pregnant. I believed her. I married her. But it turned out she wasn't pregnant. I wasn't happy but we were married and I thought we'd try to make it work. A commitment is a commitment. But then she ran away, and I filed for divorce. And I vowed never to marry again." He made a low, mocking sound. "By the way, this is a terrible conversation to be having on *our* wedding night."

Ava didn't hear that last bit, too focused on what he'd said before.

The part about Eden saying she was pregnant and Colm marrying her out of duty.

Eden had forced his hand with a pregnancy.

Eden had trapped him.

Ava exhaled slowly, understanding. "That's why you reacted to my news the way you did." Her gaze met his. "That's why we had that terrible fight the night of the accident. You couldn't believe it was happening again."

"You and I are different—"

"You can be honest with me, Malcolm! You can tell me how you felt. It would help me fill in the pieces because that night wasn't you, and me, was it? That night, and our fight, wasn't about us, but about Eden and you."

"I was angry, yes."

"Because I was just like Eden."

"You're nothing like Eden. But that night, it felt like I was being cornered all over again."

"I was trapping you."

He nodded, sighed. "I think I need a drink. Want one?" he asked her.

Ava slid off her delicate high heels and drew her legs up. "Yes, please."

"Champagne?"

"Do you have anything else?"

"Brandy."

"I'll have that."

"Good. Me, too."

For a moment, the only sound was Colm drawing out two brandy glasses and a crystal decanter from the bar adjacent to the bedroom.

She watched as he poured them both a generous splash of brandy. "I hate secrets," she said. "My father had a thousand and none were good. Mistresses, ex-wives, babies out of wedlock—"

"My life is far less interesting," Colm interrupted, walking towards her. "I only have one child and that is Jack. Our son. I would never take a mistress, or have an affair. I was with no one in the thirteen months we were apart, and would still be with no one if we weren't together now. I have a lot of faults, but I am faithful."

He handed her the brandy snifter. Their fingers brushed and just that light touch flooded her with heat.

"What else do you want to know?" he asked gruffly.

"Everything."

The dim light played off his hard, hard cheekbones and his beautiful mouth. "Narrow the field a little, would you?"

"Tell me about us," she said carefully. "Not the us of today. But the us of the night of the accident."

"I don't believe in living in the past."

"I know. But help me understand one more time that night, so that I can try to reconcile what I thought I knew, with what I've learned tonight. *Please.*"

Colm held his breath a moment, battling with himself, and his judgment. Tonight was supposed to be special. Tonight was supposed to be about his and Ava's future. But here they were, once more, battling the past.

"You and I met at a fundraiser for the ballet. I was enamored with you from the start. I took you out after a performance and we stayed in that restaurant, in that corner booth, talking for hours. Then I took you back to my place, and made love for hours and we never looked back. It worked. We worked. We were happy."

"But we didn't talk about the future, did we?" she asked.

"No."

"What did we talk about?"

Her eyes were wide and dark and very somber. Colm's lips lifted faintly. "We didn't really talk about anything. We just enjoyed each other. And we did enjoy each other." He hesitated. "But we'd also agreed to a relationship that had no strings, no rules, and no commitments."

She looked skeptical. "I don't believe that. I can't believe I'd ever agree to such a thing."

"You were career focused. Ballet was your love." He shrugged. "It's what you told me, time and again."

"And you believed that?"

"Maybe I wanted to believe that, yes. I was happy to believe that." Again his shoulders shifted beneath the crisp white shirt. "I didn't want to fall in love. My marriage with Eden was so painful, I knew I'd never marry again, so a physical, sexual, pleasurable relationship with no strings attached sounded perfect."

"That's why it was such a shock for you when I told you I was pregnant."

"Not just pregnant, but almost five months. I couldn't believe it. You were so tiny. You carried so small. I told you I didn't believe you. I told you that even if it was true, I didn't want the baby."

"Or me," she whispered.

He inclined his head. "I regret every angry word I said."

"I can understand now why you were so upset. It must

have been like déjà vu. There you are with another Eden."

"I'll never forget how devastated you were, Ava. I will never forget the look at your face as I put you in that taxi. I'd broken your heart. Shattered you—"

"Don't." She shivered. "Don't go there. It's too sad."

"But I remember it all. And as if it wasn't bad enough that I put you in the taxi, shattered, I then get a call that you're at the hospital, dying." His voice cracked. "By the time I arrived at the hospital you weren't expected to last the night. And then the doctors added that you were pregnant, close to five months, and did I want them to try to save the baby?" Pain darkened his eyes. "You hadn't been lying. You were telling me the truth. And there you were, pregnant with my son, and *dying*."

After a moment he continued. "I was desperate. I vowed that I'd do everything in my power to make sure you and the baby survived." The intensity in his eyes nearly leveled her. "And I have."

Ava inhaled at the wash of pain. They had both been through so much. "No wonder you don't like to look back. I don't blame you."

He sat down on the edge of the bed next to her, and took her hand, kissing the back of it, and then the palm, and up the inside of her wrist. "I've learned to be grateful for every day. And I count my blessings every, single day, which means I thank God for you and Jack every day, because you two are my greatest blessings."

She smiled then, a slow smile that curved her full lips and made her lovely dark eyes shine. She was beyond beautiful. She took his breath away.

"We've been through a lot, and the past three and a half years haven't been easy," he said, "but I'd do it all again if it meant we'd be here today."

He meant every word, too. He'd always found her physically appealing but now their bond wasn't just the physical. They were bonded through struggles and challenges and unexpected joys. And then there was Jack, a testament to love and life and hope.

"I love you, Ava," he said, cupping her face and lowering his head to hers. His mouth brushed her lips, and then again.

"I know."

Chapter Fourteen

THE GREAT THING about being loved by Colm, was that he was very, very good at making her feel good and beautiful. And loved.

Ava's eyes closed as he kissed her again, his lips traveling ever so slowly across hers, from one corner of her mouth to the other.

By the time he lifted his head, her heart was thundering and her body trembling. She wanted him. She couldn't imagine a time where she wouldn't want this fierce, beautiful, loyal man.

"Ava?"

There was a question in his voice but he knew what she wanted. She knew he knew.

She reached for Colm, tugging at his shirt, pulling him closer, craving more contact.

"All these clothes," she murmured. "Far too much fabric."

"You're reading my mind," he said, turning her to begin

unfastening the dozens of little hooks at the back of her fitted gown, working from the top of the bodice down. She shivered as he peeled the dress away and his lips kissed her bare back, close to her shoulder blade. He kissed his way down her spine, kissing the dip and then the curve of hip.

She felt so hot and sensitive, her skin covered in liquid velvet. He stroked her, his hands pushing the silk skirts down, freeing her legs. His hand slid between her thighs, and he caressed her, teasing her, warming her, and slowly starting to do what he did so well: drive her mad. "Love me," she whispered.

"I do, baby."

And then he was thrusting into her and showing her how much he did love her. She couldn't imagine anything feeling better than this. It wasn't merely sex, but a union of hearts, minds, lives.

She didn't want to come, didn't want the pleasure to end. But Colm was too good and the sensations too intense and when she climaxed, Colm was there with her, just as he'd been there every step of the way.

LATER, AFTER THE fire burned out and the champagne shifted in the silver ice bucket, Ava lifted her head and looked down at Colm. His blue-green eyes met hers and held. He was happy. She knew it without him saying so. They didn't need words between them, not after all they'd been through.

She felt the same happiness, as well as a great peace. She'd made it. She'd been through the fire. She'd survived and come out the other side and it was all worth it.

"Can we go check on Jack?" she whispered, running her hand across Colm's hard chest. She could feel the thump of his heart. "I know he's asleep, but I'd love to still tuck him in."

He reached up, caught her face and brought her back down to him. He kissed her thoroughly before letting her go. "I can't think of a better way to end the night."

The End

Love alpha heroes? Check out *New York Times* bestselling author Jane Porter's newest series....

Taming of the Sheenans

Christmas at Copper Mountain
Book 1: Brock Sheenan's story

The Tycoon's Kiss
Book 2: Troy Sheenan's story

The Kidnapped Christmas Bride
Book 3: Trey Sheenan's story

The Taming of the Bachelor
Book 4: Dillion Sheenan's story

A Christmas Miracle for Daisy
Book 5: Cormac Sheenan's story

The Lost Sheenan's Bride
Book 6: Shane Sheenan's story

Available at your favorite online retailer!

About the Author

New York Times and USA Today bestselling author of forty-nine romances and women's fiction titles, **Jane Porter** has been a finalist for the prestigious RITA award five times and won in 2014 for Best Novella with her story, Take Me, Cowboy, from Tule Publishing. Today, Jane has over 12 million copies in print, including her wildly successful, Flirting With Forty, picked by Redbook as its Red Hot Summer Read, and reprinted six times in seven weeks before being made into a Lifetime movie starring Heather Locklear. A mother of three sons, Jane holds an MA in Writing from the University of San Francisco and makes her home in sunny San Clemente, CA with her surfer husband and two dogs.

Visit Jane at her website, www.JanePorter.com.

Thank you for reading

The Tycoon's Forced Bride

If you enjoyed this book, you can find more from all our great authors at TulePublishing.com, or from your favorite online retailer.

Printed in Great Britain
by Amazon